SECRETS OF THE CASTLETON MANOR LIBRARY™

Bitter Words

Jan Fields

Annie's®
AnniesFiction.com

Library of Congress-in-Publication Data
Bitter Words/ by Jan Fields
p. cm.
I. Title
                                    2016961794

AnniesFiction.com
(800) 282-6643
Secrets of the Castleton Manor Library™
Series Creator: Shari Lohner
Series Editors: Janice Tate and Ken Tate
Cover Illustrator: Bonnie Leick

10 11 12 13 14 | Printed in China | 9 8 7 6 5 4 3 2 1

1

"A cat!" Mitzi Hubert shrieked, jumping back from the gorgeous walnut library table where the tuxedo cat stared at her scornfully. She held her clipboard full of papers up in front of her like a shield. "You have a cat in here."

The cat continued to hold the woman's gaze with his own, his body completely still as if he were just one of the many carvings in the huge library room.

Faith Newberry, the Castleton Manor librarian, regarded the younger woman in surprise. "That's my cat, Watson."

Taking another step back, Mitzi fanned her red face with her clipboard. "You can't have a cat in here."

"Actually, Castleton Manor is completely pet friendly. You'll find dogs and cats everywhere during your stay. I thought you knew that. It's in all of the literature you received." Faith couldn't understand the other woman's attitude. Watson wasn't menacing in any way. Sure, he continued to stare at Mitzi, but Faith suspected he simply had a wicked sense of humor, and the woman was watching him like he might go for her throat at any moment.

"You don't understand," Mitzi said, smoothing her carefully-styled short red hair and making an obvious effort to modulate her voice. "You cannot have a cat in *here*. Sugar Worthington will be bringing her two Poms, Ginger and Snap. They do not get along with cats, so that cat must be kept someplace else during Sugar's book signing. That is not negotiable."

Faith resisted the urge to sigh. Sugar Worthington's demands were beginning to pile up, and the celebrity pastry chef had not even arrived yet. *Why did I think this cookbook authors' retreat was going to be fun?* "I will leave Watson at home on the day Sugar is scheduled to do her book signing in here." Not that leaving Watson at home guaranteed that he would *stay* at home. The cat had proved adept at sneaking out of the cottage, and Faith still wasn't sure how he managed it. Faith had always known Watson was smart, but since she'd taken the librarian job at the luxury resort, the cat had developed the uncanny ability to appear at the most opportune—and sometimes inopportune—moments.

"I suppose that will have to do." Mitzi offered Faith a tight smile, finally tearing her gaze away from Watson. "As Sugar's personal assistant, I'm trying to make the experience positive for my boss and her fans. This cookbook authors' retreat is very important to her."

"And to us. Castleton Manor is also committed to giving our guests the most positive experiences possible during their stay."

Mitzi nodded and looked briskly around the two-story library. Faith followed her gaze with a certain pride. The manor's library was truly magnificent and housed more books than many public institutions. A carved walnut ceiling soared far above the room in a perfect marriage of craftsmanship and artistry. The spiral staircase that offered access to the second-floor books was a masterwork of wrought iron and carved wood all by itself. When she added in the rest of the elaborate trim around the room, the red velvet furniture, and the impossibly tall, built-in bookcases holding literally thousands of volumes, the room never failed to fill her with awe.

Small locked glass cases held some of the collection's rare volumes, though a few of the rare cookbooks lay on the reading table near her desk where Faith had been working on her own presentation for the retreat, until Mitzi arrived with all her demands.

Faith would be giving a talk on the history of the cookbook in America, and she was looking forward to it. When she read about the dishes that cooks were able to turn out with ingredients and circumstances that would have the modern cook weeping, her daily problems were quickly put in perspective.

Pulling her attention back to the present, she turned back to Mitzi, expecting to see the same awe in the young woman's face. Instead she saw a frown. "Everything in here is awfully old, isn't it?"

"I suppose so," Faith replied, measuring her words. "The house itself was built in 1895, and this library contains a number of priceless first-edition books as well as one-of-a-kind art objects. If Castleton Manor weren't a resort, it would make an impressive museum."

Mitzi nodded. "Old and stuffy. Sugar Worthington is all about new and fresh ideas in the kitchen and in life." She offered another dramatic sigh. "I suppose it cannot be helped." She looked at Faith hopefully. "Maybe we can brighten it up a little? Add some color with cushions on the seats. Put away these old books." Mitzi poked at the cookbooks and Faith quickly rescued them, wincing at the fact that she hadn't had time to slip on cotton gloves before picking them up.

"These are first-edition cookbooks. I'll be using them in my talk on the history of the American cookbook. When I'm finished, they'll be replaced in their glass cases, where they can be protected." She carried the books over to her desk and put them down gently. Watson was no longer perched on the reading table and had slipped away. She hoped he wasn't up to any mischief.

Mitzi followed. "Do you really think anyone is interested in old cookbooks? They don't even have pictures on the covers."

She turned to gesture across the room, her nose wrinkled. "Maybe you could display stacks of Sugar's book on every table instead. They're very colorful."

Faith carefully smoothed the sides of her dove-gray skirt to keep her hands from clenching. "We will have a lovely display of Miss Worthington's books ready by tomorrow, as well as a mixed display of the books by some of our other guests."

Mitzi looked horrified. "I expect the display of books by lesser cooks will be smaller and given more discreet placement. After all, Sugar is the star here."

"I'm not likely to forget that. Miss Worthington's books will be the featured item," Faith promised.

Mitzi looked back toward the now-empty library table. Though Watson wasn't there, apparently her memory of him lingered on, because the woman shuddered. "And you'll remember about the cat."

"I will, though I cannot ban guest animals from the library. If I were to do so, Miss Worthington's dogs wouldn't be able to come in either. There may be cats in here during the signing, but I can make sure Watson will not be among them."

Mitzi sighed wearily. "It can't be helped, I suppose. Still, I expect the staff to be watchful of possible pet conflicts." She lifted her clipboard and made a note. Faith assumed it was something about harassing the rest of the staff on the issue of pets. "Oh, and please do not call Sugar 'Miss Worthington.' She hates it."

"I'll be certain to remember," Faith said. "Is that everything?"

Mitzi looked around again, then offered another long-suffering sigh. "I suppose." She forced a smile. "We do what we must with what's available, right?"

"Considering what's available is a sixty-thousand-square-foot, French Renaissance chateau-style mansion and one of the premier resorts in the country, making do shouldn't be too painful," Faith said.

Mitzi looked directly into Faith's eyes for the first time. "I didn't mean to ruffle your feathers. Like you, I'm trying to do my job to the best of my ability. Sugar can be demanding. Wonderful, but demanding."

"I'll keep that in mind."

Mitzi waved her hand carelessly. "Sugar is as sweet as her name, but she knows what she likes. And I like to get it for her."

Faith nodded, but she did wonder: *If Sugar is so sweet, what was with all the demands?*

Fall had brought an end to Lighthouse Bay's long sunlit evenings, and it was already quite dark on the winding, tree-lined drive as Faith headed into town. She kept a sharp eye out for wildlife. The resort had plenty of deer and the usual collection of smaller animals. Though she couldn't see them now, she knew most of the younger trees had fencing around them to keep the deer from eating away the bark in the winter.

The velvety darkness was soothing after the day she'd had, and now she was looking forward to a much more relaxing evening. She had only stopped at her cottage on the grounds of the estate long enough for a quick dinner before jumping back into her car. As she thought about the Candle House Book Club, the group that had become her social lifeline since taking the job at the manor, she felt her tension from the day drain away. She made the rest of the drive into downtown Lighthouse Bay with a faint smile on her face.

Lighthouse Bay depended heavily on the busy tourist trade through summer and early fall and managed to bring in people, even in the icy Cape Cod winters, with unique downtown events. Though her job kept her busy, Faith made as much time as possible to enjoy the windswept beaches as well as the boutique shops, historic museums, and amazing food. The simple fact was that Faith loved her new home and her new job, even on the tough days.

Faith saw a number of people strolling along the sidewalks of the cobblestone-paved Main Street, despite the chilly fall air. The shops had not yet started keeping their shorter winter hours. She found a parking spot near the Snickerdoodles Bakery & Tea Shop and decided that was a sign she should stop in for a cream puff, a treat that had become nearly an addiction.

Faith stepped into the bakery with barely a glance at the large square room with small tables and chairs in the front; her focus stayed on the glass cases at the back, filled with fantastic treats. A few customers, none of whom Faith recognized, were seated at the tables near the cases, talking quietly between bites of pastry.

Faith inhaled scents of vanilla, cinnamon, chocolate, and brewing coffee. Finally the annoyance of dealing with Mitzi Hubert seemed far away.

"Faith!" Jane McGee, the plump, red-haired baker working behind the counter, tapped on the top of the glass. "Don't tell me. Let me guess. Cream puff?"

Faith resisted the urge to press her hands to the case like a little kid. She smiled up at the baker. "I've become horribly predictable."

"Not at all," Jane said with mock seriousness. "I'm a pastry psychic."

Faith laughed. "Finally, someone has cooking magic that our special guest at the manor hasn't claimed to have yet, at least not in the official bio I read."

"Oh, that's right," Jane said. "You're having a cookbook authors' retreat out at the manor. I wish I could come."

"Are you working on a cookbook? Most of the retreat guests are working on cookbooks they hope to publish, though I know we have a few who already have a cookbook out, but want to learn new skills for future books. We're going to have talks about cookbooks, cooking techniques, and even a few on publishing. I could see about getting you a day pass, if you're interested."

"That's so kind. But I mostly want Sugar Worthington's autograph. I have two of her cookbooks. I love her and her show, but I need to stay here and meet the pastry needs of the desperate citizens of Lighthouse Bay."

Faith smiled. "You're a true humanitarian. The book signing will be in the manor library. I can get you a signed copy of the new cookbook if you like."

Jane's face lit up. "You'd do that? In that case, this cream puff is on the house." She quickly bagged up the fluffiest one in the case, and Faith carried the treat next door to the Candle House Library.

As always, Faith admired the beautiful stone building that housed the privately-funded library. The three-story building was compelling in its simplicity; its quiet beauty came from the blues, grays, and soft browns of the stone, as well as the clean lines of the building's design. Originally, it had housed the town's small candle-making industry, until a proper candle factory was built at the far end of Main Street in the 1840s.

Inside, the building had been completely renovated to serve as Lighthouse Bay's library. Because of their private funding, the Candle House Library didn't suffer from the budget pinches that were biting libraries all over the country. Faith walked into the softly lit main room, her boot heels ringing on the hardwood floors. She headed straight for the impressive fireplace. The fireplace, where tallow was once processed, now served as the focal point for the library's seating area. The comfy, upholstered chairs were mostly full.

Patting the empty chair beside her, Midge Foster waved Faith over. Midge was the busiest person Faith had ever met. She was a veterinarian and owned Happy Tails, a gourmet pet treat bakery. She was also married with two kids in college.

As Faith slipped into the seat, she spotted a tray of cream puffs on the coffee table near the chairs. "Now I feel guilty," she said, holding up her bag. "I brought my own."

Midge grinned, her green eyes sparkling. "You made a wise call. The way this group goes after cream puffs, it's every woman for herself."

Faith reached out to pet the tiny Chihuahua in Midge's lap. Atticus was the only dog in the book club, and he was terribly spoiled as a result. It didn't hurt that he was also adorable since Midge tended to dress him up in seasonal outfits. Tonight he wore a black bow tie with pumpkins printed on it. The oversize glasses the little dog wore to correct his vision problems added to his whimsical cuteness.

"So where's Watson?" This question came from Faith's aunt, Eileen Piper, who sat on the other side of Faith. As usual, she had her most recent knitting project in her lap, an afghan in warm fall colors destined for the harvest raffle at the church. Eileen was the head librarian at the Candle House Library. A kind-hearted and positive person, she'd been a huge source of support as Faith settled into Lighthouse Bay.

"I was going to bring him, but he pulled one of his mysterious disappearing acts right after he wolfed down dinner," Faith said. "I think his feelings were hurt. Sugar Worthington's personal assistant came by today to deliver her boss's list of demands about the cookbook authors' retreat, and she acted like Watson had rabies."

Midge harrumphed. "I can vouch for Watson. He is completely up to date on his shots."

"That personal assistant is horrible," Brooke Milner snapped, gesturing with the cream puff in her hand. "If Sugar is half as annoying, this is going to be a long week."

Brooke could always be counted on to stick up for her friends, but this time Faith suspected there was more to it than that. Brooke was a sous-chef at the manor and often fielded requests for specific dietary needs.

"I take it you met her?" Faith asked.

"She came by the kitchen and nearly had the head chef ready to fillet her by the time she was done. She actually questioned the cleanliness of the kitchen. *Our* kitchen. There are operating rooms that are less clean than the kitchen at Castleton Manor."

"Mitzi summed the library up by calling it 'old,' so I'm not surprised by anything she might have said. Maybe we'll discover that her boss is nothing like her. Mitzi did say Sugar was sweet." As Faith leaned back in the cozy chair and crossed her legs, Atticus scrambled across Midge's lap and put his feet up on the arm of the chair, clearly looking for more attention. Faith reached over to rub the top of the little Chihuahua's head, receiving a friendly lick in return.

"Saccharine is sweet too, and completely artificial. I can't say I'm looking forward to the circus when the diva herself sweeps in," Brooke said, punctuating the comment with a savage bite into one of the pastries.

"I'm going to try to keep a positive expectation," Faith said. "It's better for my nerves, which needed some serious downtime after spending the afternoon with Mitzi. I hope that will be the most challenging part of this retreat, and the rest will be smooth as the filling in this cream puff."

Brooke snorted, clearly doubting reality would match up to Faith's hopes.

Eileen set her knitting project in her lap and smoothed it with one hand. "I have to admit, I'm looking forward to the book signing."

Faith raised her eyebrows in surprise. "You're coming?" She knew her aunt was far more into gardening than cooking. In fact, Eileen was part of the Lighthouse Bay Garden Club and almost single-handedly kept up the Victorian garden at Castleton.

Her aunt nodded as she continued fidgeting with a wayward strand of yarn. "I've baked a number of Sugar Worthington recipes, and they've always come out perfectly. Plus, I am a huge fan of her reality show, *Sweet & Sassy*. I don't think I've missed an episode since it first premiered."

Faith continued to stare at her aunt, unsure of what to say.

Brooke filled the gap. "I've caught an episode or two, but there wasn't enough eye candy for me. They never get into any romantic entanglements. You'd think someone like Sugar would have some kind of steamy romance going."

"Well, I'm impressed with anyone who can keep private things private in today's reality television world," Midge said as she straightened the pumpkin bow tie that Atticus had knocked cockeyed when he'd tried to scramble over the side of the chair.

"I've actually been a little worried about Sugar," Eileen admitted, gently smoothing the curling edges of the afghan. All eyes turned to her in surprise.

"Worried?" Faith echoed. Not only did her aunt apparently watch reality television, but she also actually *worried* about the people. Faith knew, of course, that Eileen was kindhearted, but this was definitely a surprise.

"I take it you don't watch the show." Eileen paused as Faith shook her head. "Sugar has lost a lot of weight over the course of filming. I'm concerned that the network is forcing her to conform to some ridiculous beauty standard. She looked perfectly fine before, curvy but fit. Now she's very thin."

"Maybe she's been ill," Midge suggested. "Or maybe she's trying to eat healthier. I know I am." She cast a rueful look at the cream puff tray, and Faith suspected she'd already had one.

"The demanding menu that Mitzi turned in certainly didn't seem very healthy to me," Brooke said. "And it didn't suggest Sugar is dieting either. That woman apparently doesn't eat anything that isn't buttered or fried."

"Her new book is titled *Butter Won't Kill You . . . Too Quickly*, so I suppose she's trying to live up to the title," Faith said, but the conversation left her curious. What would the pastry diva be like in real life? If Eileen liked Sugar, or at least her television persona, Faith was willing to give her the benefit of the doubt. She supposed she'd find out soon. Hero or villain, Sugar Worthington would be descending on them in the morning with her film crew in tow.

Check-in day for the cookbook authors' retreat started so pleasantly that Faith was almost ready to set aside her misgivings from the day before, especially when early guests began wandering into the library, some of them still dragging luggage since they'd arrived ahead of official check-in times. The manor staff was more than willing to hold the luggage until they could carry it up to the rooms, but some guests were hesitant to leave their things.

Without exception, the face of every guest lit up with the same awe Faith felt over the massive library. Each time she showed off the library's extensive cookbook collection, the new guests gasped. Faith wondered how many meals someone could prepare using the manor's cookbooks without ever duplicating one. She filed the thought away to research sometime. It would be a fun fact to add to her library presentations.

Not long before lunchtime, one of the writers at the retreat, a slender young woman with a cascade of black hair, tapped Faith lightly on the arm to get her attention. She pointed toward the upper-level balcony. "Are there any cookbooks up there?"

Faith shook her head. "No, the cookbooks are all shelved together except for the ones on display." She gestured toward the new displays set up specifically for the retreat.

The young woman's face fell. "All right. Thank you."

Faith offered her a conspiratorial smile. "You're welcome to go up there anyway. The view looking down on the rest of the library is amazing."

A smile broke over the woman's face like a sunrise over the Atlantic Ocean. "Thank you." She rushed across the room to climb the ornate spiral stairs. Faith couldn't blame her. She'd been known to create reasons to go up there herself, simply to look over the wrought iron balconies.

When a quiet moment came, Faith walked to the French doors that led outside, enjoying the play of the low October sun on the tiles of the terrace. They'd been enjoying unusually warm days lately and the thought of sitting in the sunshine was tempting. She made a mental note to have her lunch there later.

Finally she turned away from the windows and drifted out to the Great Hall Gallery. She loved the bustle of check-in day for any event. It was always fun to watch people discovering Castleton Manor for the first time. Like everything about Castleton Manor, the gallery was opulent, with platinum-leaf wall panels, marble and alabaster accents, and urns filled with gorgeous greenery to bring life to the room. On the library end, a statue of Agatha Christie looked down on the crowd with a calm eye. All along the outside wall, tall French doors offered magnificent views of the ocean.

Shouts and high-pitched barks drew Faith's attention toward the other end of the gallery where Sugar Worthington was sailing in, her arms full of two yapping Pomeranians. A cluster of people followed in her wake, including several men carrying huge cameras and other impressive-looking equipment.

The celebrity pastry chef had a thick mane of blonde curls, artfully styled to look effortless. She wore a Dresden-blue turtleneck sweater with a draped scarf in exactly the same shade. Her winter-white wool skirt was alarmingly tight, and Faith suspected Sugar would have had trouble walking if the skirt hadn't been so short. She had to admit, it showed off her long legs and the suede boots with spike heels that made the arches of Faith's feet ache in sympathy.

Faith saw Mitzi Hubert trotting along beside Sugar, her shorter legs clearly making it difficult to keep up with the chef's stride. Mitzi reached out to show Sugar something on her clipboard and one of the little dogs snapped at her, making Mitzi jump back. "No wonder she's so nervous," Faith muttered.

All around the cavernous space, guests snapped pictures of Sugar with their phones, while professional photographers called out the pastry chef's name. When she paused and turned to each with her signature bright, friendly smile, the camera flashes made the whole event look more like a red carpet premiere than a guest speaker checking in at the resort.

Sugar finally swept out of the room and up the grand main staircase with her entourage following. Faith turned to head back to the library. She was nearly through the long gallery next to the library when a lanky, carrot-topped man in a suit barreled toward her, carrying an easel and a huge photo of Sugar. Sugar's big blue eyes stared guilelessly out at Faith.

"Oh excuse me," the man said when Faith jumped out of his way. "I didn't see you. I have to get this set up in the library before Marlene notices it's not up yet."

Faith felt a rush of sympathy for the man as he hurried on into the library. She'd dealt with Marlene Russell, Castleton Manor's assistant manager, plenty of times, since Marlene was technically her boss. She was often demanding and somewhat inflexible. Faith had given up on getting Marlene to like or appreciate her.

When Faith entered the library in the young man's wake, she watched him set up the easel near the display of Sugar's cookbooks. "How does it look?" he asked fretfully. "Does it grab your attention?"

"Without question," Faith said. She stood and looked at the photo for a moment, trying to imagine her own face blown up to that size. She doubted her blue eyes would look quite as doll-like.

The man thrust a hand out at Faith so suddenly she almost jumped. "Cole Venn," he said. "I'm new. Well, newish. This is my first big event. I work in publicity."

Faith took his hand, surprised to feel calluses, proof that Cole wasn't a stranger to hard work. "I'm Faith Newberry," she said, "the librarian."

His expression changed to one of alarm and he began babbling. "Oh, I'm so sorry. I should have introduced myself out in the gallery and asked where you wanted this easel. I didn't know you were the librarian. You don't look like one at all."

"The easel is fine right where you put it," Faith assured him. "And what does a librarian look like?"

He paused, obviously thinking about it. "I'm not sure. More like Marlene, I suppose."

Faith thought of Marlene's sharp features, perpetual scowl, and her fondness for wearing her hair in a tight bun. "I don't know any librarians who favor Marlene's style," she said with a smile to show she wasn't offended. "Most of the ones I know look a lot like me."

He smiled in return. "Then I should hang out in more libraries." He took a moment to brush nonexistent dust from his neatly pressed clothes, then drew himself up very tall. "I have to run. I have one more poster to put up next to the hostess podium in the Banquet Hall. I should have had these up yesterday. Marlene is totally on the warpath. Nice to meet you." He rushed out the door before Faith could say anything in response. She turned back to the poster, checking to be sure it didn't obscure the books on the library table behind it.

"Is this the library where Sugar will be signing books?"

Faith turned to see a plump woman with a head of tight black curls clutching one of Sugar's older cookbooks. "Yes," she said. "But not today. The only scheduled event on check-in day is the mixer tonight."

"Oh, I know," she said, her tone still a little breathless as her gaze swept past Faith to the display of cookbooks. "That poster is amazing. I would love to have that."

Faith looked at the poster, trying to imagine wanting to look regularly at it. "Really?"

"Of course. Sugar is my hero. Well, she's the hero for a lot of us pastry chefs. She's done so much to bring attention to our art form. And she's so real and warm and down-to-earth."

"You've met her?" Faith asked.

The woman's eyes widened, clearly surprised. "No, not yet. Though I hope to, at the signing. You can really see the kind of person she is from watching her show."

Faith rather doubted that. She suspected reality television was a long way from real, but she certainly didn't want to argue with a guest. As she thought about the size of the entourage she'd witnessed, she doubted the young woman's assessment of Sugar was exactly accurate. "I think she'll be at the mixer," Faith said. "And she'll definitely be giving some talks as well as doing the book signing. You'll see all the times and locations in your packet."

"I haven't had a chance to read that yet. I will though," the young woman said, her gaze never leaving the display. "Am I allowed to look at these?"

"Sure," Faith said. "And we have an extensive vintage cookbook collection." Faith slipped smoothly into her description of the books while the starstruck young woman bobbed her head in response.

When the young woman had finished looking at all the cookbooks and left to explore the rest of the manor, Faith looked over at her desk, thinking she really should put some time into reviewing the materials for her own presentation. Maybe she should eat her sandwich at her desk, though then she couldn't touch any of the books until her lunch was finished.

Although it was clear she wouldn't inspire the kind of glowing adulation that Sugar did, she did want to give an engaging and interesting talk. Now that the hullabaloo was dying down, she should be able to put in a few hours of work.

A shout drew her attention to the open double doors of the library. Someone was yelling in the gallery beyond, and Faith was fairly certain she recognized the voice. She walked over and peered through the doorway.

Under the statue of Agatha Christie, Marlene Russell stood nearly nose-to-nose with a man Faith didn't recognize. The assistant manager's hands were on her hips and she looked as if she were considering driving her rather pointed nose into the man's eye. "That is completely unacceptable."

"You know, you're lucky to have someone of Sugar Worthington's stature show up at some out-of-the-way Cape Cod resort." The man crossed his arms over his chest, making his biceps bulge under the sleek brown sweater he wore with a copper-colored scarf and one of the soft knit hats that seemed to be essential apparel for the modern hipster. Faith's gaze swept down to the slightly short hem on the man's slacks, which showed off expensive-looking loafers and bare ankles. *Who goes without socks on Cape Cod in October?* Even with the warm days they'd been enjoying, the thought made her shiver.

Marlene's voice jerked Faith's attention away from the man's clothing choices. "Castleton Manor is a premier luxury resort, not some hole-in-the-wall motel. We booked Miss Worthington. We are merely tolerating you and your collection of television people." She made "television people" sound like an insult.

"It's a package deal, lady," the man said. "Sugar is under contract for *Sweet & Sassy*, and this is the last episode of the season. It needs to be spectacular, and that means we need to see promotional posters for Sugar in every shot."

"No." Marlene's voice made it clear she wasn't budging. "I have agreed to posters on easels in prime locations. That is all. If you want a poster in every shot, then you must limit your shots to places where the posters already exist. Castleton Manor's reputation for elegance and style will not be compromised."

"I'm not asking you to put up neon signs."

"Elton, what is going on?" Both Marlene and the man turned sharply to face Sugar Worthington, who strode down the gallery with her arms full of squirming dogs. "You know Ginger and Snap don't like all that negative energy. It upsets their systems, and I don't want to have to take them to a strange vet."

"No negative energy here, Sugar darling," the man drawled. "I'm trying to explain our filming needs to Mrs. Bussell."

"That's Russell," Marlene snapped. "And I prefer *Ms.* Russell. I also prefer to avoid making Castleton Manor look like a circus sideshow with tacky banners and screaming carnival barkers."

"Of course you do," Sugar cooed. "And I'm sure my producer didn't mean any harm. He can be a little overzealous when it comes to promoting the show. I wouldn't want you to do anything that makes you uncomfortable."

"Sugar," the producer said, his tone unhappy.

"Elton, don't scold." Sugar pouted as she walked the last few feet and shoved one of the little dogs into his arms. Since the dog didn't snap at him, Faith assumed the Pomeranian liked the producer more than it liked Sugar's personal assistant, Mitzi. "I have a splitting headache, and I happen to agree with Ms. Russell. This place is gorgeous and viewers are going to want to see it exactly the way it is."

The producer's frown didn't lighten, but he did pet the little dog, which settled into his arms as if it spent a lot of time there.

Faith could practically see Marlene's feathers unruffling. "I'm glad to see you're being sensible about this," Marlene said, turning to exclude the producer from her comments. "We have some lovely posters up in the library and the Banquet Hall where you'll be introduced tonight."

"Oh, a banquet hall," Sugar enthused. "I'd love to see it." She expertly steered Marlene away from the fuming television producer who stood in the long gallery with the Pomeranian in his arms for a moment before trailing along behind the two women.

Faith turned back to the library and her lunch. The rest of the afternoon was spent showing off the library collection to still more guests. Clearly, it was going to be a well-attended retreat.

"And this display," she said to an attentive group who looked around the room eagerly, "is made up of cookbooks by our other presenters and even a few of our guests at this retreat."

The round-faced young woman who'd been carrying around one of Sugar Worthington's books earlier now looked at the second display and said wistfully, "I would love to have a cookbook of my own to display. I've been collecting recipes from my family for years and I'm hoping to learn enough at this retreat to finally turn them into a real cookbook. My grandma Mimi makes a blueberry buckle that's to die for."

A short man with a pinched look about his face spoke up from the edge of the group. "You need to be careful to guard that collection."

"Guard it?" the woman said.

"Yeah, don't show the recipes around, not even to people you think you can trust." The man's tone was bitter. "You never know who will take the chance to steal from you."

"Steal recipes?"

"Recipes, dreams, your future." With each word, the man's tone grew angrier until he turned to glare back toward Sugar's poster. "It's all the same to some people."

"You can't mean Sugar." The look of shock on the young woman's face was clear, then the look turned into stubbornness. "She'd never do anything like that. She happens to be a personal hero of mine."

His face softened slightly at that. "Be careful who you idolize. Be careful who you trust. It's often the biggest idol that has feet of clay." With that, he turned sharply on his heel and stalked out of the library, leaving the rest of the group murmuring after him.

3

"Who do you think he was talking about?" The Sugar Worthington fan had lost all of her bright eagerness after talking to the strange man. Even her curls seemed to droop. She swung her tote bag up into her arms and hugged it as she turned to Faith. "Do you think it's safe for us to bring our cookbook projects here?"

"Of course it is," Faith said, tentatively patting the woman on the arm. "As a librarian, I've read about literary theft, and it's really quite rare. Most of the time similarities in books are coincidental."

The slender woman who'd climbed the stairs to the second-floor balcony twisted a strand of her long black hair nervously. She lowered her voice. "Rare isn't the same as never. I left my recipes in my room. Now I wonder if I should have put them in the safe. You don't have room break-ins here, do you?" Her eyes darted to the door.

"I assure you, your project is perfectly safe in your room," Faith said.

Despite her continued assurances, the group soon trotted out of the library, nervously whispering to one another. Faith watched their retreating backs and had the gloomy suspicion that somehow their worries were going to come back to haunt her, especially if Marlene heard about the incident.

With the library empty, Faith was about to continue work on her presentation when she caught a flash of movement outside the tall French doors leading to the tiled terrace. She detoured over to the door and groaned as she caught sight of Watson looking back at her. She opened the door. "You're supposed to be at the cottage."

The cat peered through the opening, leaning forward slightly to bring his nose to the very edge without coming through. "Come on," Faith said. "Or I'm going to leave you out there." The cat continued to stare into the room, his tiny stump of a tail twitching until Faith began to ease the door closed, which prompted Watson to dart in.

Faith closed the door and scooped up the black-and-white cat, nuzzling the top of his head. "You're lucky you're so cute. Now try to stay out of trouble, Rumpy. We'll be going home in a couple of hours."

Watson blinked at her innocently, then butted the top of his head against her chin. She carried him over to her desk and settled down with the cat in her lap while she pulled on cotton gloves so she could look through the antique cookbooks. She wanted to check one last time to be certain she had every recipe marked that she planned to read from during her talk. Watson apparently didn't find her lap appealing once she stopped petting him, and he jumped down to the floor to settle on top of one of her feet.

After an hour of reading through her notes and making little tweaks to the presentation, she was interrupted by a pair of guests, each clutching a worn binder to her chest. "We're going to some of the cookbook writing workshops this week," the taller of the two women said.

"And we wondered if we really need to worry about recipe theft," the second woman added. "My recipes have been in my family for generations. A few even came over on the *Mayflower*."

"Mine too. Well, not the *Mayflower* part, but the generations part is definitely true."

Faith sighed and slipped her foot gently out from under Watson so she could stand. She walked over to smile at the two women. "Literary theft of any kind really is quite rare," she repeated. "I don't think you have to worry about an offhand comment made by one guest."

The women seemed only slightly reassured, and Faith decided to try for distraction instead. She led them to the cookbook section, and both were soon happily gushing over the unique books in the collection.

The brief lull appeared to be over, and the rest of the day passed quickly with people coming and going from the library frequently. A few brought in pets on leashes or in their arms, but Watson paid the furry guests little attention, which Faith appreciated. She had enough trouble calming plagiarism fears without pet battles as well. It seemed most of the visitors had picked up the nervous jitters from the earlier incident. When Faith finally closed up the library for the day, she was positively beat.

She scooped up Watson and headed out onto the tiled terrace where pools of light marked the fact that dusk had come while Faith was inside. To her surprise, she saw the terrace was in use. Sugar Worthington sat on one of the marble benches in the shade of the overhanging balcony above.

Hesitant to interrupt the woman's quiet contemplation of the gardens beyond the terrace, Faith considered slipping by without speaking, but Sugar settled the question for her. "Hello there. I saw you this morning," she said, her voice spiced with a bit of a drawl. "You were in the gallery when I was smoothing my producer's ruffled feathers."

"I was," Faith said. "I didn't mean to eavesdrop, but the gallery is the only way to get from the library to the main entry unless I walk around the outside of the building." Plus, the arguing had caught her attention, but Faith decided not to add that part.

Sugar waved off the implied apology. "Those two were going at it like cats and dogs. It's no wonder you'd want to have a look. Are you a guest at the retreat or do you work here?"

"I'm the librarian," Faith said. She gestured back toward the French doors. "The library is through there. That's where you'll be doing your book signing."

Sugar nodded. "I'll have to have a peek. If you're the librarian, you must be the one giving the talk on antique cookbooks tomorrow. I'm looking forward to that one. I'd like to include more traditional recipes in my next book, recipes with real history to them."

As she spoke, Watson squirmed in Faith's arms until he managed to jump free. When he hit the ground, he trotted over to rub against Sugar's calf. "Oh, I'm so sorry," Faith said, reaching for the cat. "Your assistant told me to keep Watson away from you."

Sugar waved her off. "Nonsense. I adore cats, and this one is a cutie. Is he one of those tailless breeds?"

Faith shook her head. "I found him when he was a kitten on the streets. He'd lost his tail in some accident. The poor thing was skinny and sick. It was touch and go for a while. Luckily Rumpy is made of tough stuff."

"Rumpy?" Sugar said. "I thought you said his name was Watson."

Faith laughed. "Rumpy is a nickname, and if I didn't know better, I'd say he hates it." Based on the disapproving looks the cat was giving her from his spot next to Sugar's leg, she almost would have thought he understood English.

"That's so funny." Sugar gestured to the seat beside her on the bench. "Please, do sit and chat for a few minutes. I rarely get a chance to talk to anyone without a camera in my face."

Faith wasn't sure what she had expected from the celebrity chef, but the graciousness definitely surprised her. She smoothed her skirt and sat down on the bench. "It must be exhausting. I saw you arrive, and it looked positively overwhelming."

Since Sugar had stopped petting him, Watson took the opportunity to pad to the edge of the terrace where he could sit in the soft glow of one of the terrace lights and begin a long grooming session. Faith watched him, wondering if she should pick up the cat so he wouldn't disappear later when she was heading for the cottage.

"Celebrity can be a blessing and a curse," Sugar said, pulling Faith's attention back to her. "Don't get me wrong, I appreciate my fans. Without them I'd be an ordinary Georgia baker with big dreams. But I do like my private times too."

"And now I'm intruding." Faith started to rise but Sugar reached out to catch her arm.

"No, you're sharing it with me." She looked back toward the French doors to the library. "Do you have a lot of old cookbooks in there?"

"Old and new both, including yours," Faith said. Then her mind went back to the incident with the angry man earlier in the day and all the fretful guests who'd come in afterward. "Some of the guests today were worried about protecting their recipes. Is there a lot of literary theft in the cookbook world?"

Sugar's smile vanished and her warm tone chilled. "What are you implying?"

Faith scooted slightly away from the pastry chef, alarmed by the extreme change in her tone and demeanor. "I'm not implying anything, honestly. It's something a few guests asked me. I've read that literary theft is less common than people think, but I really don't know much about the cookbook publishing field specifically."

Sugar's expression remained guarded. "Well, first of all, recipes are considered formula, so they aren't protected by copyright. They're only lists of ingredients and lists of directions for using them. So a basic recipe can't be stolen in the legal sense."

"Oh . . . right." Faith remembered something about lists from an intellectual property class she'd had in college. "So if someone did publish someone else's recipes, there wouldn't be much the original author could do about it."

Sugar shrugged. "Baking and cooking are like comedy, I suppose. Someone is always stealing your best material. But in reality, few of us are really the creator of our recipes. We're all building upon techniques and ingredients and traditions that are part of our cultural landscape. In my cookbooks, it's the stories I share about my favorite recipes that make them unique more than the food itself."

Faith nodded. When she'd been preparing her talk, she'd thought about how much the directions for each recipe and the introductions to them revealed about the history of the times in which the food was popular. And even the oldest cookbooks sometimes included commentary that gave insights into the times and the people. "That makes sense."

Sugar visibly relaxed and smiled again, though not nearly as warmly.

The cat paused in the careful attention to his fur. He believed perfect grooming was essential to his dignity, and he believed in dignity at all times. He looked casually toward his human and the stranger

who smelled faintly of dog. He didn't hold the smell against the poor woman. Many humans seemed fond of the slobbering, silly creatures.

Suddenly, movement on the second-floor balcony caught his attention. He looked up sharply, hoping for a plump bird. But the movement was only another human holding a flowerpot. He squinted. He didn't understand the human preoccupation with putting plants in pots and then not chewing on them. It didn't even look like a tasty plant.

Above him, the human pressed against the balcony rail, leaning the heavy pot on the edge. The cat glanced from the pot to the women below. He didn't like the look of that.

How dare someone endanger his human! This was bad—very bad. The cat leaped to his feet, his fur on end. He pointed his nose at the balcony and cried out with all the volume he could muster.

At the horrific caterwauling, Faith and Sugar jumped automatically to their feet.

"Watson, what's wrong?" Faith dashed across the terrace with Sugar right on her heels. They had only gotten a few steps away from the bench when they heard the crash. Both spun to look in horror at the large ceramic flowerpot, broken on the bench where they'd been sitting moments before. If Watson hadn't yowled, they might have been killed!

4

Faith looked up at the small balcony that overhung that portion of the terrace and caught a flash of movement. She was certain someone had ducked out of sight, but the movement was far too quick for her to recognize anyone. Still, someone had clearly been on the balcony when the flowerpot fell.

She turned to the chef beside her and noticed the woman looked pale. "Are you all right?"

Sugar shuddered slightly. "I had a moment there where my imagination ran away with me. If your cat hadn't yowled . . ." Her eyes widened. "Where is your cat?"

They both turned toward the stairs again where Watson sat calmly, meticulously licking his paw. Sugar rushed over and scooped him up. "There's my hero." She launched into a stream of baby talk that had Watson staring at her in what Faith imagined was a mixture of horror and disgust.

Before she could say anything to rescue her cat, people began pouring up the steps, coming to see what had made the loud crash. A mix of guests and workers from the resort, the crowd was soon caught up in Sugar's charm as she cuddled Watson and described his rescue in glowing terms. As much as Faith appreciated her cat, she wasn't sure he deserved quite so much applause for simply being noisy.

It wasn't long before Marlene Russell showed up. Faith stifled a groan. *I knew it was too much to hope she'd gone home for the day.*

The slender woman stomped across the terrace, sputtering with rage. She pointed sharply at the mess of dirt and pottery shards. "Where did this come from?"

"I believe," Sugar drawled, "it fell off that balcony up there, and nearly smashed my head in. If this darling kitty hadn't saved me, I wouldn't be here to talk to you now." She returned to baby-talking at Watson, making kissing noises in the cat's face. Faith was impressed that Watson hadn't scratched her by now.

Marlene took one look at Watson, then turned sharply to Faith. "And what were you and your cat doing out here?"

Faith refused to let the abrasive woman get a rise out of her. "Heading for home."

"I asked her to sit with me for a bit," Sugar insisted. "And her cat saved me. You should give them both medals." Faith almost laughed aloud at the expression on Marlene's face in response to Sugar's suggestion.

Sugar's voice lost some of its warm tone when she added, "I certainly hope y'all won't be putting any more flowerpots on the balcony up there. It's not safe."

"You're correct. It's not safe," Marlene agreed, her face darkening at the implied criticism. "Which is why no flowerpots are ever displayed on the second-floor balcony. It is completely against the rules."

"Then what do you call that?" Sugar asked, gesturing toward the mess on the terrace tiles. "Because where I come from, we call it a flowerpot."

"And I will track down whoever made such a dangerous mistake in direct violation of the rules. I assure you, that person will not be in a position to make that mistake again."

Sugar gently put Watson down on the terrace, then stood and pressed her hand to her stomach, waving Marlene away with her other hand. "You do whatever you like, but all of this is simply too upsetting. I'm going to go upstairs and lie down a bit before dinner." Sugar swept through the crowd like a queen, clearly expecting people to get out of her way as she walked. Faith was impressed with the pastry chef's outward display of calm, though she also noticed Sugar still looked pale.

Marlene stepped closer to Faith, thrusting her pointed nose at her like a disgruntled bird. "Do you have anything to add?"

"I thought I might have seen someone on the balcony," Faith said. "But the person darted out of sight too quickly for me to be sure."

"Was it anyone you recognized?"

"I don't know. Honestly, it was more an impression than a clear look. Whoever was up there moved very quickly."

Marlene sniffed, quickly dismissing Faith's input. "Or else you imagined it. Okay, you can go. I'll handle this."

Not wanting to extend her time with Marlene, Faith was happy to take that as her cue to leave. She scooped up Watson and carried him down the stairs, heading for the cottage and a nice quiet cup of tea. Stroking the cat's fur as she wove her way through the gardens, she thought about the falling flowerpot. Watson leaned against her, purring, and she tugged his ear gently. "How is it that you're always in the middle of trouble?" If he had an answer, he showed no sign of it, merely purring with his eyes closed.

The long walk to the cottage was calming with the sound of the ocean in the background. Faith passed through the gardens and meandered among the topiaries. Since it was October, the flowers were mostly gone and the green of the topiaries had turned slightly golden. The gardeners had brought out pots of mums to fill in color in all the beds. They set off the reds and golds of the surrounding autumn trees beautifully, and Faith soon felt as if she were leaving the near accident far behind.

As she left the Victorian garden, she finally caught sight of her destination. That first glimpse of the stone gardener's cottage was always the best part of the walk for her. The cottage was easily both the most historic and most beautiful place in which Faith had ever lived. Plus, she could still hear the ocean, crashing against the rocky shoreline beyond the thick stand of trees. She still sometimes had to pinch herself as she opened the beautiful arched door so she would know she wasn't dreaming that this was her home.

As soon as the door opened, Watson squirmed to be put down. He didn't waste time gawking at the ambience. Watson was all about the chow, and he began meowing so that Faith would know how important it was to feed him at once before he starved to death.

"You could have stayed home and snacked on kibble all day," she scolded mildly as she unwound her soft pink scarf and hung it on the coatrack near the door. "So I have no sympathy for you."

Watson bumped her ankle with his head and meowed again. She gave in and headed for the kitchen to feed the cat and herself. When both were full and content, Faith decided a cozy fire and a little reading would be the perfect way to end the day. As she knelt in front of the hearth and began the process of laying the fire, her mind went back to the incident on the manor's terrace.

Had she really seen someone up on the balcony? She'd certainly had the impression of movement and color. *What color? Something rusty red, maybe? Could the person have had red hair?* She really wasn't sure, but that was the sense she'd gotten. Her mind immediately flashed to Sugar's redheaded assistant, Mitzi, but she brushed it aside, scolding herself firmly for looking for a mystery in a simple accident. *I probably just want that tiresome assistant to be guilty of something besides annoying everyone.*

When the fire was burning merrily, she heard a knock at the door and opened it to Brooke Milner's cheerful face. "I finally finished for the day and I had to get the scoop from you on the Sugar Worthington crisis. Did someone really try to drop a flowerpot on her?"

"Come on in," Faith said, stepping away from the door. "I don't have many exciting details, but I was there and the flowerpot did fall from the second-floor balcony." She waved a hand toward one of the comfy chairs facing the fireplace. "Can I get you something? Coffee? Tea?"

"Nothing for me, thanks," Brooke said as she curled up in the chair.

"I'm going to grab a yogurt for dessert," Faith said. "My stomach is still a little jumpy from my near-death experience. You sure you don't want one?"

"Do you have blueberry?" Brooke asked. When Faith nodded, she smiled. "Okay, I'll have one, thanks."

Faith brought two small yogurt containers and spoons. She sat down in the chair next to Brooke and handed over the yogurt. "You sure you don't want anything else?"

"Now you're just torturing me. I want details. The gossip machine was going in the kitchen, but you never know how much to believe. Did you really push Sugar out of the way?"

Faith laughed as she peeled off the top of the container and Watson hopped up onto her lap, clearly hoping for a chance to lick the lid. "Hardly. I came about as close to getting conked on the head as she did and was just as clueless. I'm sure the falling pot was simply an accident."

Brooke turned her head toward Watson. "I also heard Watson pushed you out of the way of the falling pot, but I was betting on you."

Faith burst out laughing and put the lid on her knee. "Honestly? Watson pushed me to safety? He's an impressive cat, but he's not a lion."

"I said I heard it, not that I believed it. Though one of the bellmen was totally sure that he heard Watson was the hero."

"I suppose he was, in a way. Watson was caterwauling for some reason. I never did figure out why," Faith said. "Sugar and I went to see what was upsetting him, and the pot fell right at that moment."

"So the really important question is, did someone try to drop a flowerpot on Sugar or you?" Brooke asked, her eyes sparkling with mischief. "Who was the intended target?"

"I really don't think it was intentional at all." As Watson finished lapping the yogurt from the lid, Faith set it onto the side table and stretched her legs out so she could feel the warmth of the fire on her feet. "I'm sure it was one of the newer staff who didn't know the rule about not putting plants on the balcony. We have flowers everywhere else, so I suppose it's a reasonable mistake. Now the person is too scared of Marlene to come forward and admit to being the one who nearly killed our guest speaker."

"You can't blame them. Marlene is scary. Too bad we're not having a big Halloween party. She could come as the witch."

"Bad idea," Faith said as she turned to stare into the fire. "She'd scare the guests. You know, I did think I saw someone on the balcony right after the pot fell."

Brooke froze with a spoonful of yogurt almost to her mouth. "Really? Man or woman?"

Faith shook her head. "I couldn't tell. Honestly, all I really saw was movement and maybe some color. The person *might* have been a redhead."

"I knew it!" Brooke's enthusiastic outburst made Faith jump. "It was Mitzi. That's what I thought all along. She totally seems like the scheming murderer type to me."

"Really?"

Brooke's smile turned mischievous. "No, but you have to admit that she's a perfect suspect. You practically caught her red-handed. Or red-haired." She popped the spoonful of yogurt into her mouth.

"That's a bit of a stretch. I don't even know for sure what I saw."

"It's not a stretch. After dealing with Mitzi Hubert yesterday, I could totally picture her dropping a pot on someone. Plus, no one on the planet loves their boss as much as she pretends to. I'm telling you, it was her."

"Wouldn't dropping a pot on Sugar's head put Mitzi out of a job?" Faith asked. She took a bite of her own yogurt.

Brooke pointed at Faith with her spoon. "Don't rain on my theory with logic. Though really, if the pot had nearly beaned Mitzi, you'd have a much longer suspect list. She managed to annoy half the staff." She leaned forward. "Did you talk to Sugar? Is she as much of a diva as she sounded from Mitzi's demands?"

"She was nice to me, though I suspect she isn't always as sweet as her name," Faith said. "We didn't talk long."

"I guess we'll find out by the end of the week," Brooke said as she leaned back in the chair and joined Faith in staring at the fire while they ate the rest of their yogurt in silence. After that, the conversation turned to less sensational topics for a while until Brooke popped up and announced she needed to be getting home. After she left, Faith returned to watching the slowly dying fire. As much as she'd sounded sure when she talked to Brooke, she still felt uneasy about the accident. *Just how accidental was it?*

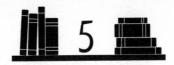

5

Holding up a rather plain, clothbound book with frayed corners, Faith smiled out at the cookbook authors filling most of the seats in the library. "Early cookbooks are known for their long titles." She opened to the title page and read aloud, *"American Cookery, or the art of dressing viands, fish, poultry, and vegetables, and the best modes of making pastes, puffs, pies, tarts, puddings, custards, and preserves, and all kinds of cakes, from the imperial plum to plain cake: Adapted to this country, and all grades of life."* She paused several times while getting through the title to take a dramatic breath, making the audience chuckle. "Published in Hartford, Connecticut, in 1798, this wasn't the first cookbook printed in America, but it was the first written by Americans for Americans. The book includes recipes using New World ingredients such as corn, cranberries, turkey, squash, and potatoes. So this book set the stage for what all of you are doing today, bringing unique recipes to the people who want them."

"Is that a first edition?" a heavyset man in one of the closest chairs asked.

"No, but close," Faith said. "We do have several first-edition Early American cookbooks." She reached for one just as something crashed at the other end of the room, making everyone jump.

Faith gave the film crew an annoyed glance. A broad-shouldered, bearded man with a roll of cable in his hand had backed into one of the marble plinths that held the brass filigree lamps providing light for the library, sending the lamp crashing to the floor. Luckily, those lamps were probably the least valuable items in the library. "Did the lamp survive?" she called.

The man righted the lamp and shook his head as the upper part of the lamp dangled loosely. His cheeks above his beard pinked. "I'm sorry, miss."

Faith turned back to her audience. "Apologies," she said, forcing a smile for the people surrounding her. "Technical difficulties."

"Are we going to be on *Sweet & Sassy*?" Faith recognized the round-faced fan with the head of curls from the day before.

"Not at this talk," Faith said. "They're setting up for Sugar Worthington's book signing directly after lunch. I hope you'll all come back for that." She held up the small cookbook again to draw the group's attention back to her presentation. "A unique aspect of this recipe book was the author's use of pearl ash as leavening for dough. Pearl ash came from the plentiful wood ashes in early American kitchens. It was in common use in the colonies by the time of this publication, but it soon became a revelation to cooks worldwide."

Though no one knocked over any more lamps, the noise from the film crew was constant and Faith saw people turn to look at them many times as she tried to hold their attention with her presentation. Finally, in exasperation, she called out. "I'm nearly done here. Do you suppose you could hold off the rattling and banging until the end? Since you're in the film business, I'm sure you appreciate the value of a big finish."

The crew looked sheepishly at one another and the bearded man who'd spoken to her before said, "No problem. We'll wait." They all backed away from their equipment and leaned against the library wall with arms crossed.

Faith launched back into her talk and was glad to see the men stand respectfully still and quiet as she spoke. Finally, the audience seemed to find the topic as interesting as Faith herself did, and no one else turned to look at the back of the room. The only person sneaking looks in that general direction was Faith herself. She kept glancing toward the library doors, expecting to see Sugar. Apparently the celebrity chef's interest in early American cookbooks wasn't as sincere as it had seemed the day before.

As she closed the last book and slipped off her gloves, she smiled at the guests. "So you can see that you're all part of an innovative, unique history filled with heart, creativity, and good eating."

After a smattering of light applause, the guests began gathering their things. Faith called out, "Don't forget, there is going to be a demonstration of new cooking technology in the salon, beginning in thirty minutes."

At that, most of the people hurried out, but a few walked over to compliment Faith on her presentation. Some even asked about specific recipes she'd mentioned. "Although you're welcome to manually copy from the older books in our collection with the proper safeguards, you can actually find the contents of many of these cookbooks online. They've been digitized through Feeding America: The Historic American Cookbook Project. You'll find information about it in the handout I gave you."

As each one of them quickly pulled out the handout, Faith saw the producer for *Sweet & Sassy* storm into the library. "What's going on?" he demanded in a roar, waving his arms for emphasis. "You aren't being paid to stand around and gawk."

The guests surrounding Faith turned to watch the drama, and Faith walked across the library to rescue the film crew. "I asked them to hold off until I finished my presentation," she said calmly.

The producer turned to glare at her. "And you are?"

"Faith Newberry, the librarian for Castleton Manor. The resort's guests paid for the full retreat experience, including the ability to hear my presentation on early American cookbooks."

He turned to look over his crew, who were trying to both appear busy and watch the pending tirade from their boss. "You are all working for the librarian now?"

While the crewmen shifted nervously, Faith spoke up, pulling the producer's attention back to her. "While I know all of you have an important job to do, you really need to keep in mind that while you are here, your film crew must not ruin the enjoyment of our guests here at Castleton Manor. I can go and get Marlene Russell to explain that to you, if you like."

The mention of Marlene's name had the intended effect, and the producer settled down considerably. "There is no reason to bother *Ms.* Russell. Now that you've explained what happened, I'm glad the crew stood around doing nothing so you could finish. I'm certain we can be set up in time for Sugar's signing in spite of the delay."

Faith surveyed the producer. As before, he wore a scarf and matching knit hat, though today's version was a muted blue-gray. He also wore black-rimmed glasses with the clearest lenses she'd ever seen, making her suspect they were more fashion than function. "I'll be sure to tell Marlene how obliging your crew has been," she said sweetly.

The producer seemed unsure how to take that, so he paused for a moment, then offered his hand. His tone finally changed to something civil. "Please excuse my manners. I'm Elton Fritsch. I'm the producer for *Sweet & Sassy*. I know I can be a bit of a pain, but I actually am glad the crew is working well with the staff here."

Faith shook his hand, which was cool and smooth. "I'm sure it must be difficult to produce a show in so many different locations."

"Reality television is actually much more difficult and more creative than people realize." He then launched into what promised to be a long-winded treatise on the artistic validity of reality television, and Faith had to stifle a groan. She'd almost rather he keep yelling at her. She pasted what she hoped was an interested look on her face until the bearded man from the crew rescued her by calling Fritsch over to deal with some mechanical issue with one of the cameras.

Though she needed to put the cookbooks away, Faith ducked out of the library to discourage Fritsch from launching back into the lecture about reality television. She decided to go outside to the front terrace and take in some fresh air for a few minutes. As she walked down the long gallery hall, she suddenly caught sight of a flash of black and white at the end of the gallery. "Watson?" she called. Surely the cat wasn't wandering around the manor on the very day she'd been asked to keep him at home. She picked up her pace. "Watson!"

The cat, if it was a cat, disappeared into the main hall. By the time Faith reached the huge open space, the cat was nowhere to be seen. Faith still wasn't certain that she hadn't imagined the glimmer of black and white, but she didn't want to risk it. She walked through most of the huge downstairs rooms, keeping one eye out for Watson and the other for Marlene. She was sure her boss would have something to say about her being so far from the library, but she had to find the cat before he got both of them into trouble.

Her efforts proved depressingly fruitless. In the music room, she saw two of the women from the morning cookbook presentation, admiring the carved red-oak wall paneling and the hand-sculpted marble mantel. Faith crossed the room to ask them if they'd seen a cat wandering around.

As she approached, she heard one woman change the topic of the conversation from the room to the resort's guest star. "I can't believe Sugar wasn't at breakfast this morning. We were promised that she'd be available throughout the retreat week. I'm simply dying to meet her."

"Did you notice she left the meet and greet early yesterday?" the other woman complained. "If I don't get to speak to her at all, I'm going to be so disappointed."

Faith decided against bringing up her search for Watson when the women were not in the best of moods. She didn't want them to think she was trying to distract them from their concerns. "She'll be at the book signing today after lunch," Faith said. "I'm certain you'll be able to meet her then. Are you coming to that?"

"Yes," the first woman said as the other one nodded. "But that's really not the same as schmoozing. And no one has seen her today."

The woman's comment reminded Faith of her surprise at Sugar missing the cookbook talk. She had a brief flashback to the falling flowerpot and her worry increased substantially. Although it would definitely be overstepping her job title more than a little, Faith wanted to check on Sugar and make sure she was all right.

Faith knew Sugar was in the Jane Austen Suite. She'd overheard Marlene grumbling about it. It was one of a number of things Mitzi had insisted upon: a tour of all the suites so she could pick the one that best reflected Sugar's *essence*.

Faith walked back through the main entry and started up the wide, sweeping staircase. The two largest suites on the second floor were the Agatha Christie and the Jane Austen, so it was no surprise that Mitzi would have chosen one of those two for her boss. One of the resort's fancy, gold-lettered Do Not Disturb signs hung on the doorknob.

Faith kept her eyes on the sign for a moment. She was painfully aware that coming up to Sugar's room was outside her job description, and knocking on a door with that sign dangling from the knob cranked it up to "serious offense" level. She took a step back, but then the memory of that heavy pot smashing against the bench came back to her again. She took a deep breath and knocked lightly on the door. To her shock, the door moved inward. It wasn't completely closed.

She pushed the door, opening it a crack, and called, "Miss Worthington? Sugar? It's Faith, the librarian from yesterday. I saw the sign on your door, but I was worried. Are you all right?"

She heard a whining sound, but that was all. Hesitantly, she pushed the door a little more. Then to her horror, Watson appeared from out of nowhere and darted by her legs, squeezing through the crack and into the room. Inside, she heard a single sharp yap from one of Sugar's little dogs.

"Miss Worthington," Faith said, pushing open the door and walking in. "I'm so sorry about Watson. I had no idea . . ."

For an instant, she stared, frozen. Sugar Worthington lay sprawled next to the ornate French Regency writing desk. Both of her little dogs were tucked in around her, looking woefully up at Faith.

6

The Jane Austen Suite was soon a whirl of contrasts. The opulent French Regency decor with its sumptuous fabrics and lavish details seemed an odd setting for so much motion. Emergency workers poked and prodded Sugar, who remained unconscious even when they loaded her onto a stretcher.

One of the resort staff, a somber-faced young woman, snapped leashes on the two little dogs, who watched their mistress and shivered miserably. And in the middle of the bustle, Faith stood with her arms wrapped around herself, feeling overwhelmed by the whole situation, not able to take her eyes from Sugar. She'd been terrified when she found her lying so still on the floor. Only the slow rise and fall of Sugar's chest, proving she was breathing, had kept Faith from complete panic. Even now, her stomach clenched with nerves and she almost groaned aloud when Marlene Russell detached from the group hovering around Sugar and stalked over.

"How is it that *you* found Miss Worthington?" she demanded. "This is a long way from the library."

Faith stood her ground. "Yesterday, Sugar told me she was looking forward to my talk on the history of the cookbook in America," Faith said. "But she didn't show. And I heard guests talking about her having missed breakfast. I was worried."

Marlene thrust her head forward, looking once again like an aggressive bird with her pointed nose and narrowed eyes. "It wasn't your job to worry about Sugar."

The shock that had coated Faith's emotions up until then began to thin, and annoyance replaced it. "I wasn't worried because of my job. I was worried about Sugar."

"You ignored a Do Not Disturb sign."

Faith held up her hand, tired of dealing with Marlene's abrasiveness. *Why doesn't she ever let up?* "I did what seemed appropriate at the time, and now Sugar is getting medical treatment, which she clearly needs. Now, I need to go back downstairs to deal with the postponed book signing."

Marlene opened her mouth, clearly intending to snipe at Faith some more, but then she snapped it shut and stepped back to make way for Faith to pass. Faith gave her a sharp nod and looked quickly around for Watson. She certainly couldn't leave the cat in Sugar's suite. She spotted Watson near the edge of the platform where the room's lavish king-size bed was situated. He was barely out of reach of the two little dogs who strained against their leashes in an effort to reach him. Faith shook her head. If there was trouble to be had, it seemed Watson was quick to find it.

The cat spotted his human moving toward him, but he wasn't done showing the two silly ragmops who was really the boss of the castle. He especially liked the strangled noises they made as they lunged against their leashes. A cat would never make such a spectacle of himself.

A cat also would never let his human confuse him with one of those ridiculous dogs that came when they were called or did tricks for kibble. He waited until his human was bending over to grab him, then he darted across the room and under the writing desk.

Peering out from under the desk, while his stump of a tail twitched, he considered the next place where he could run to prolong the chase. He would let his human pick him up eventually, of course, but only after he'd showed her that it must be his choice.

He backed up slightly, moving farther under the desk in case his human was considering dragging him out. His tail end smacked against something under the desk, making the thing roll. The cat caught the scent of sugar and something else, something wrong. He didn't like having the bad smell so close to him so he batted the thing with his paw and watched it roll out into the room.

As the thing moved, it suddenly looked interesting again. The cat followed it, giving it another swat. He was so interested in the rolling that he failed to notice his human until she'd scooped him up.

Tucking the cat into one arm, Faith bent to look more closely at the thing he'd been chasing, quickly recognizing it as a chocolate truffle with a small bite taken out of it. She grabbed a tissue from the box on the writing desk and used it to pick up the candy. Was Sugar eating that when she collapsed? It seemed likely since she surely wouldn't have left chocolate on the floor where the dogs could get it.

She looked over at Ginger and Snap, who had collapsed into a panting heap when they couldn't break free of their leashes to chase Watson. Why hadn't the dogs eaten the piece of candy? If Watson could find it, they could have as well, and she knew dogs loved chocolate, even though it would make them horribly sick.

The little dogs must have been so worried about Sugar that they simply ignored it. They had been pressed closely to Sugar's sides when Faith found them.

"I thought you were in a big hurry to return to the library."

Faith quickly slipped the tissue-wrapped chocolate into her blazer pocket. She'd dispose of the chocolate downstairs where it couldn't hurt any of the resort's furry guests. She forced a neutral tone, as it wouldn't improve the situation to argue with Marlene. "I'm going right now."

"Good." Marlene turned away from her immediately and called out to the young woman who stood over the two panting dogs. "Take Ginger and Snap down to the dog spa for the works. I don't want them left up here where they can chew on the furniture or worse."

"Yes, Ms. Russell." The young woman practically curtsied as she hurried out the suite door ahead of Faith with the little dogs prancing along beside her.

Faith was barraged by guests almost as soon as she stepped into the library, and she was reminded again how fast gossip travels when fingers fly over cell phone keyboards. Of course with gossip, speed and accuracy rarely went together.

"Is it true that Sugar killed herself?" The distraught fan clutched a copy of Sugar's recent book. "I knew I should have asked her to sign this last night."

Faith stared at the woman for a moment, then forced a smile as she set Watson down. "Sugar did not kill herself. She had some kind of health issue. She's being treated and I'm sure we'll hear more details soon."

Another guest pressed close to Faith and whispered loudly. "The health issue thing is a cover-up, right? Was it another murder attempt? Like the flowerpot?"

"The flowerpot was an accident," Faith said firmly, though she had her doubts. "And the incident upstairs is medical. I'm sure Sugar is going to be fine."

Faith raised both hands and spoke more loudly to be heard by the entire group. "Obviously Sugar Worthington's book signing has been postponed. We don't have any definite answers about her collapse at this time, but she is receiving excellent treatment. I'm certain she will appreciate your concern when she has recovered."

Her statement didn't stem the tide of questions, and so Faith patiently answered each guest with vague, encouraging comments.

A middle-aged man whose belly strained the buttons of his navy blue blazer pointed a finger at Faith. "The resort is trying to hush this all up. That's why you won't give us any straight answers."

"I'm telling you all the answers I know," Faith said in what she hoped was a soothing manner. "It's simply too soon to know what caused Sugar's collapse. I'm sure the doctors will be looking at her medical history."

An older woman with gray curls spoke up from the back of the group. "I bet it's some kind of crazy starvation diet. I always suspected the network insisted she lose weight, and now she's made herself sick. It's disgusting what the media forces on young women."

"We really don't have any answers yet," Faith repeated, though she wondered if the woman had hit on a possible answer. She remembered her aunt's concerns about the chef's recent weight loss. But what if it wasn't a diet? What if Sugar was actually ill? She'd seemed fine when she arrived. Faith gave herself a mental shake for engaging in speculation like the group of fans in front of her.

"May I have everyone's attention?" Cole Venn strode over to stand beside Faith. The lanky young man held a long strip of paper with *Postponed* printed on it, and he looked over the crowd with a solemn expression. "We have asked for regular updates on Miss Worthington's condition, and we *will* let you know what we know as soon as we know it. I'm confident that the book signing will soon be rescheduled. In the meantime, there will be a special presentation on event catering by our own sous-chef, Brooke Milner, in the salon directly after lunch." He looked down at his watch. "Which is being served right now."

At that, the library quickly cleared out, and Cole stuck the strip of paper across the huge poster of Sugar. Then he responded to the few remaining questions with confidence. As soon as the stragglers gave up asking for information that no one had, Cole turned to Faith and wiped imaginary sweat from his brow. "That went as well as could be expected," he whispered. "I'm off to put out the next fire."

"Thanks for the save," Faith whispered back.

"If you should see Ms. Russell, feel free to tell her how efficient and amazing I am." With that, he gave her a quick smile and rushed out.

Suddenly finding herself in an empty library, Faith sagged slightly in relief, but the feeling was short-lived as she pictured Sugar lying on the floor. She assumed it was a bad sign that the pastry chef hadn't regained consciousness before they whisked her away to the hospital.

She shook off the image and focused on the state of the library. Though the guests had mostly been quizzing Faith and Cole, they had still managed to make a mess of the cookbook displays and to pull a number of books from the shelves. Faith turned her attention to tidying up the library in preparation for the afternoon. She figured she would probably have more guests in and out between workshop sessions.

Before she began, she remembered the piece of candy in her

pocket. She shoved her hand in, hoping the chocolate hadn't begun to melt in the warm library, and sighed in relief when she saw it was still intact. She carried it over to the ornate brass wastebasket near her desk, but somehow she wasn't sure she should throw it out. She stared at the tissue-wrapped bundle in her hand for a moment, then impulsively put it in the drawer of her desk.

"I'm probably being silly," she whispered. She pushed the drawer shut, determined to shut up her concerns along with it, and began to put things right in the library.

As she pulled a book out of the arm holding the globe, she was reminded of how many interesting places guests managed to leave books. With so many tables, why would anyone shove a book into the globe's frame? She turned the book over in her hands. It was one of the small vintage cookbooks, though not a valuable one. She leafed through it, thinking how glad she was that building a fire was no longer a normal step in soup making.

"Oh, there you are."

Faith looked up to see Mitzi hurry in, looking more than a little frazzled. "The library is where I usually am," Faith said.

"Of course." Mitzi offered her a bright smile. "But I'm thankful that you don't always stay in here, since you've rescued Sugar twice now."

"I didn't rescue Sugar on the terrace. Watson rescued both of us."

"Watson?" Mitzi tilted her head quizzically, so Faith gestured toward the cat sitting on the rug nearby. "Oh, the cat, right. I'm surprised he's here today, since Sugar was supposed to have her signing."

Faith indulged in a brief fantasy about Watson rescuing her again by leaping up and clawing the annoying assistant, but the cat seemed disinclined to do anything but sprawl on the rug, so

Faith settled for being coolly professional instead. "I brought Watson to the library after the signing was postponed," she said, which technically wasn't a lie. "Did you have something you needed?"

"Oh no, I only wanted to tell you that Miss Worthington and I are grateful for your help."

Faith raised her eyebrows. "Sugar is awake?"

"Yes, and she would appreciate it so much if you'd come to see her at the hospital." She seemed to force her smile a little brighter. "After work, of course."

"Do the doctors know why Sugar collapsed?"

Mitzi dropped her voice to a whisper, despite the fact that they were the only people in the huge library. "They're still running tests, but the fact is that Sugar has been having a teeny-tiny problem with her stomach lately. You know, being a star is stressful. I'm sure it's related to that." She pressed her finger to her lips. "But mum's the word. We can't have the fans thinking Sugar's own cooking gave her stomach problems."

"I won't be engaging in idle speculation about Sugar's condition," Faith said. "And I'll be glad to visit her after work. I was very worried."

"I'm sure she'll appreciate that."

A group of guests walked in and Mitzi jumped away from Faith, probably making their conversation look far more clandestine than it had been. The group drifted over to the display of Sugar's cookbooks, where they promptly began messing up Faith's careful arrangement.

"What are you doing here, Andrew?" Mitzi demanded, storming over to the table. For an instant, Faith thought the woman was simply overreacting to the disarray of the display, but it was soon clear that Mitzi's upset was more personal. It was directed at a specific guest, the man who'd started the buzz about literary theft. Since the man wasn't very tall and Mitzi was wearing heels, they stood nearly nose-to-nose. She glared fiercely at him.

"I'm a guest at the retreat," he said mildly.

His calm tone seemed to upset Mitzi even more and her voice rose nearly to a shout. "Where you're not allowed to be, and for good reason. Sugar has a restraining order, as you well know!"

Faith stiffened at the news that Sugar had a restraining order against one of the guests. Apparently Sugar was far from universally loved. She considered calling security, but so far only Mitzi's behavior was agitated.

"This is a cookbook authors' retreat, and I'm a cookbook author," he answered, his calm demeanor sloughing off and his volume climbing as he spoke, making Faith slip her hand into her pocket in preparation for calling security if necessary. "As *you* well know, I've been working on my cookbook of classic Old West recipes for years, right up until half the recipes were stolen."

"You better watch your mouth!" Mitzi yelled back. "I'm going to get someone to enforce that restraining order, and now that I know you're slinking around here, I'll have the cops check out where you were when a flowerpot nearly smashed Sugar's head."

As it turned out, Faith didn't need to make the call to security. The yelling had brought in the ground-floor security guard who normally strolled casually around, keeping his eye on the valuable art displayed in every room. The guard looked to Faith. "Any problems, Miss Newberry?"

It was Mitzi who answered. "This man shouldn't be here. Throw him off the property."

"I'm a registered guest!"

The guard was clearly in over his head and looked toward

Faith. "They should probably talk to Marlene," she suggested. She knew Marlene would be furious if Faith took it upon herself to have a guest removed. And, in all fairness, it was Mitzi who seemed to start the altercation, though the words "restraining order" were more than a little concerning.

The guard gave Faith a pained look, but he gestured toward the gallery. "If you both will come this way, please, I'm sure we can sort this out."

"Both of us?" Mitzi asked. "I'm not the one violating a restraining order."

"And I'm not the one stealing from other authors," the man snarled.

The other guests watched the exchange raptly, and Faith could only guess how the gossip would spread about this drama. *And what if this man has already tried to hurt Sugar? What if that little accident was only the beginning?* She walked over and put a hand on Mitzi's arm. "You should go with the guard," she said gently, hoping a display of calm would defuse the situation, at least a little, "so you can explain all this to Marlene in private." She stressed the word "private" slightly, cutting her eyes toward the avidly listening guests. Surely Mitzi didn't want to feed gossip about her boss.

Mitzi shrugged off Faith's hand and turned sharply to glare at her. "Mind your own business." Faith pulled back, shocked at Mitzi's transformation to vicious shrew.

Then Mitzi pointed at the young man. "And you stay away from Sugar." She stormed past the guard and down the gallery.

"Gladly!" the man shouted after her, before turning in the opposite direction and marching outside through the terrace doors.

The guard looked back and forth, then turned to Faith. "Should I go after one of them?"

Faith shook her head. "We don't want any more of an incident than we've had." *In this public space*, she added mentally. "But you should report this to Marlene right away." *And let her have this angry guest rounded up in the privacy of his room where other guests don't get to watch.* Faith pushed a pleasant smile onto her face. "Thanks for your help."

The guard nodded politely and quickly left, while Faith turned to answer the flurry of questions left in their wake.

7

By the end of the day, Faith was certain she'd exhausted every possible way to answer questions with no actual information. As much as she loved her job, she left the library with genuine relief, wrapping her arms around herself to ward off the chill in the air. For once, Watson seemed perfectly willing to behave as he trotted along at her feet all the way back to the cottage. Along the way, she wondered if Marlene had the angry guest looked into. Faith could picture how unpleasant Marlene would be if Faith asked her about it. Surely she'd taken care of it, given the whole issue of the restraining order.

After feeding Watson and herself, Faith cast a longing look toward the cozy chair near the fireplace. She would have loved to kick off her shoes and spend the evening with a good book, but instead she pulled on a heavier jacket and headed outside. With the falling darkness, the air had turned from crisp to cold and Faith pulled the wool jacket closer around her with a shiver as she hurried to the car.

At the hospital later, her thoughts spun back to Sugar on the floor of her suite. Faith had been so worried, especially when Sugar wouldn't wake up. "But she did wake up," she reminded herself firmly, pushing the troubled thoughts out of her head and instead thinking about her cookbook presentation instead. It was the one thing that had gone well all day.

Faith found absolute chaos at the nurse's station when she exited the elevator on Sugar's floor. The *Sweet & Sassy* producer, Elton Fritsch, was having an intense discussion with a woman in hospital scrubs.

"Sugar Worthington's contract grants us access to any important incidents in her life," Elton insisted. "You cannot keep us out of her room."

The woman put her hands on her hips. "You're wrong there. I can and will. Your contract does not trump hospital rules. The patient needs to rest, and you and your bunch look anything but restful."

The producer crossed his arms over his chest and looked down on the woman. "I want to speak to your supervisor."

She smiled sweetly up at him. "I *am* the nursing supervisor."

While the two glared at each other, neither willing to budge, Faith slipped around them and headed for Sugar's room. She rapped on the door frame with her knuckles as she stepped in. "Miss Worthington?"

To her surprise, she found Sugar sitting up in bed, her hair styled and her face perfectly made up. But the even bigger surprise was the handsome man standing next to the bed, smiling warmly down at the pastry chef.

"Faith!" Wolfe Jaxon said, turning the same warm smile in her direction. Faith knew Wolfe was in charge of overseeing a number of Jaxon family businesses, including Castleton Manor and its library and literary retreat. He occupied the entire third floor of the manor when he was in town. "I didn't know you knew Miss Worthington."

"Now, y'all," Sugar drawled, swatting playfully at Wolfe. "You both need to call me Sugar. I don't need any of that 'Miss' business."

"I met Sugar yesterday," Faith said. "On the terrace beside the library."

Wolfe raised his eyebrows in surprise. "So you were there for the broken flowerpot incident."

"She was," Sugar said, laying a hand lightly on Wolfe's arm. "Her darling little kitty—I believe his name is Watson—saved us both. And Mitzi said that Faith is the one who found me today. She is a treasure. I hope y'all know that."

Faith noticed Sugar's drawl had become considerably more pronounced since their chat on the terrace, and she wondered if the chef was laying it on a little thick to charm Wolfe. It wasn't as though Faith couldn't understand it. With his thick, dark hair peppered with gray and his tall, athletic build, Wolfe was extremely attractive, and he was undeniably rich, one of the most sought-after bachelors in Lighthouse Bay and probably most of the rest of New England. Faith suspected he regularly had women vying for his attention, which was one reason she made it a point not to take Wolfe's occasional displays of interest in her too seriously.

To her surprise, Faith found that understanding Sugar's behavior didn't make her like it any better. Since she had no business being jealous of Wolfe's attention to anyone, she shook off her ridiculous reaction and took a few steps closer to Sugar. "I'm certainly glad to see you looking so well." Now that she stood at the chef's bedside, she could see the dark circles that makeup hadn't completely hidden under Sugar's eyes.

"I'm so sorry for all the fuss," Sugar said, batting her eyelashes at Wolfe before turning back to Faith. "Do you know what happened to Ginger and Snap? I must have scared my poor babies half to death, passing out like that."

"Last I heard, they were enjoying a spa day," Faith said. "They are certainly faithful little dogs. I found them snuggled right by your side when I walked into your room."

"They are my darlings. It sounds like they'll be spoiled rotten when I get them back. I won't be able to do a thing with them," Sugar said with a light laugh.

Faith debated whether she'd stayed long enough to fulfill her duty. She debated whether she should bring up the argument she'd witnessed with Andrew and Mitzi, but then decided it really wasn't her place. Marlene would not appreciate Faith jumping over her chain of command to inform Wolfe, and though Faith wasn't cowed by her boss, she wasn't necessarily eager for a Marlene moment either.

And she really wasn't enjoying seeing Sugar flirt with Wolfe, especially when he showed every sign of enjoying the attention. She tried to come up with a polite reason to escape, but before she could stammer out an excuse, they heard another rap on the door. This time it was Andy Garris who walked in. Lighthouse Bay's chief of police didn't believe in doing his job entirely behind a desk, but he wasn't usually the first officer on a scene. Faith wondered if his presence was because of Sugar's celebrity status or the prominence of Castleton Manor and the Jaxon family in the community.

The chief tipped his head slightly at Faith as he passed her and greeted Wolfe politely, then held out a hand to Sugar and introduced himself.

"My my, Lighthouse Bay certainly seems to have an abundance of handsome men," Sugar said as she held his hand a little longer than was strictly necessary.

The chief was a former marine who had stayed in good physical condition after turning to police work. He wisely ignored Sugar's flirting, merely smiling slightly. "Miss Worthington, do you know of anyone who might mean you harm?"

Faith waited for Sugar to bring up Andrew, but she merely looked at the chief with wide blue eyes.

"Harm? Why would anyone mean me harm? I'm a pastry chef."

"And yet, it appears there have been two attempts on your life in the last twenty-four hours."

"Surely you're joking," Sugar said. "The flowerpot was an accident. And I've been having a little tummy trouble lately, so I've not been eating like I should. I'm sure that's why I fainted."

The chief's sharp blue eyes shone with intelligence and kindness. "I'm afraid it's more serious than that. You didn't faint. The doctors tell me you were poisoned."

Faith gasped. "The truffle!"

All eyes turned to her, but before Faith could say anything more, Sugar spoke up, a bit louder than necessary. "Poisoned? That is ridiculous."

"As Miss Newberry apparently noticed as well, we found a box of truffles on the writing desk in your suite," the chief continued, his deep voice a gentle rumble. "There was one truffle missing. I assume you ate that one?"

"I only took one dinky little bite," she said. "But it tasted bad so I spat it out in my hand. I was heading for the wastebasket to throw it out when I fainted." Her face took on a look of alarm. "My babies! Ginger or Snap could have eaten the candy once I fell. Someone needs to take them to the vet immediately!"

"They didn't eat the candy," Faith said quickly. "I found it. I picked it up so the dogs couldn't get to it. It's in the drawer of my desk at the library. I don't know why I saved it. It seemed like a good idea, in case anyone wanted to see it."

Faith felt her cheeks warm when Wolfe looked at her in admiration. "Good thinking."

"Good thinking, indeed," the chief agreed. "I'll need that."

"We'll get it to you," Wolfe told him.

"Miss Worthington," the chief said, speaking gently, "where did the truffles come from?"

She shook her head. "I don't know. They were on my table when I got to my room." She shrugged. "When I travel, I usually have complimentary fruit or candy or flowers in my room. I didn't think much about it." She smiled slightly, though it had none of the sunny brightness Faith had begun to associate with the chef. "I really shouldn't eat chocolate with my tummy trouble, but I thought a tiny bite wouldn't hurt." She laughed dryly. "I guess it bit back."

"You need to take this attempt seriously," the chief said. "This could have ended far worse than it did."

The weak smile slipped from her face. "I still cannot believe anyone would want to hurt me. I'm a pastry chef. This must be some kind of misunderstanding. Maybe the candy was for someone else?"

The sad hope in Sugar's voice made Faith's heart go out to her, but it was clear Sugar wasn't being realistic. A woman who had taken out a restraining order on someone must know she was capable of making enemies. She opened her mouth to mention the restraining order, deciding she'd just deal with Marlene's animosity later, but the chief spoke first.

"That seems unlikely, but we'll look into every possibility. I really would like you to think about anyone who might be upset with you or carrying a grudge about anything."

"Against me?" Sugar said, batting her lashes. "I can't think of a soul."

"I have a few possibilities for you."

They all turned to find Mitzi in the doorway. Her normally sleek bob was in disarray and her red hair stood around her head like a fiery halo. "If you want to know who was mad enough at Sugar to want her dead, I can give you a list."

8

As everyone stared at Mitzi, Sugar laughed. "And people say I'm overly dramatic. Mitzi, honey, how could you possibly come up with even a single person who wants me dead? I don't have any enemies."

Mitzi crossed the room, speaking to Sugar as if she were a child. "You're always trying to see the best in folks, and I try to shield you a good bit, but there are angry people." She looked directly at the chief and thrust out her hand. "I'm Mitzi Hubert, Sugar Worthington's personal assistant."

"And official worrywart," Sugar said. "She's being silly now. No one has any reason to hurt little ol' me."

Mitzi turned to look at Sugar, her face serious. "Andrew Ashe."

"Isn't Andrew the name of the guest you were arguing with earlier? The one mentioned in the restraining order?" Faith asked, knowing full well it was. She was curious to see Mitzi's reaction, but Sugar spoke first.

"Andrew is at the retreat?"

Chief Garris looked sharply at each of them. "I'd like to hear about this Andrew and about the argument Miss Newberry mentioned."

"I don't know about any argument, but the situation with Andrew is a misunderstanding." Sugar looked down at her lap, weaving her fingers together nervously. "Simply a misunderstanding."

"I'm going to need a better explanation than that," the chief said. "You have a restraining order against this man?"

Mitzi cleared her throat, pulling attention back to her. "Andrew Ashe worked for Sugar for a while. Actually he was an intern."

"More like a protégé and a friend," Sugar said softly. Then she seemed to give herself a mental shake and looked up into the chief's face. "Andrew is a little miffed at me, yes, but he wouldn't try to *kill* me. We're practically family."

"But you have a restraining order against him," the chief said.

Sugar sighed. "I should never have let Mitzi talk me into that. If I hadn't, Andrew would probably be over it by now."

"Over what? Why is this man miffed at you?" the chief asked. Faith wondered the same thing.

"Andrew wants to be just like me," Sugar said, her bright smile back. "Which is what a protégé does, of course. He has this cookbook he wants to get published, and I was helping him bring a little life to the recipes. Readers like to get glimpses of the author behind the cookbooks, you know? I was helping him learn how to tell stories with his cooking."

The chief frowned. "And this created a problem?"

"Not exactly." Sugar shifted slightly in the bed, clearly uncomfortable with her recitation. "Andrew felt that some of the recipes for my new cookbook, *Butter Won't Kill You . . . Too Quickly*, were just a smidgen too similar to recipes in his own collection."

The chief raised his thick eyebrows. "You used recipes that belonged to your intern?"

No wonder Andrew was upset, Faith thought.

Sugar frowned and crossed her arms over her chest. "Chefs take their inspiration from all over. Do you know how often cookbooks contain truly original recipes? Almost never. It's not like Andrew created those recipes. Besides, recipes aren't copyrighted because they're basically formulas. It's the stories you tell that make them different. I didn't touch Andrew's stories."

"Just his recipes."

"A couple, maybe." She huffed in annoyance. "My publisher

was yelling about deadlines and contracts. I'd fallen a little behind because of my tummy problem. I used a few of Andrew's recipes for inspiration."

"So this Andrew is upset with you for stealing his recipes."

Sugar flinched. "Stop saying that word. I didn't *steal* anything. Besides, Andrew is really a sweetie at heart. We would have worked things out eventually."

"Sugar," Mitzi snapped, "you need to wake up. He trashed your office. He threatened you publicly. You *had* to get that restraining order. You weren't going to work things out."

Sugar shrugged and turned her shoulder toward Mitzi. "Some things take time." She smiled in Wolfe's direction, clearly preferring to direct her comments toward him. "Chefs are passionate people, but all that anger doesn't last. We kiss and make up. It'll be fine. We're like family, I tell you. Family doesn't kill each other."

"Actually, family is the first place we look in a murder investigation," the chief said as he pulled a notebook and a short nub of a pencil out of his pocket. He wrote for a moment while everyone watched him in silence. Then he looked up at Mitzi. "You want to tell me who else is on your list?"

"There's no one," Sugar protested. "Honestly, y'all are being silly."

Neither Mitzi nor the chief even glanced in her direction. "Part of my job," Mitzi said, "is to keep track of Sugar's online forums. I answer questions and keep everyone updated on her appearances." When she paused, the chief made rolling motions with his pencil to get her to keep going, his expression serious. "The discussions on the forums can be intense."

"But they're all fans of the show," Sugar said. "They love me. None of them would do anything to hurt me."

Mitzi patted Sugar's arm, giving her barely a glance. "Sugar has always been a kind of spokesperson for loving the skin you're in and not needing to conform to media standards of beauty. But now she's lost some weight, actually quite a bit." She paused and glanced at Sugar before continuing. "Well, some of her fans are feeling betrayed. We have some angry posts on the forum and a few through e-mail. Some of them get nasty and there have been a few threats."

"If only I could tell them I'm not on some crazy crash diet," Sugar wailed. "That would settle everything. I still believe in being proud of who you are."

The chief looked at her, his pencil poised over the paper. "Why not tell them?"

Sugar sighed dramatically. "The network and my publisher insist. I have to keep my illness a secret."

"What exactly is your illness, Miss Worthington?" he asked. She dropped her eyes and mumbled something unintelligible, so the chief repeated his question.

"IBS, if you must know," she snapped. "I have irritable bowel syndrome, though where I come from, a lady does not talk about her bowels. At any rate, almost everything I eat makes me sick. It's awful." Faith felt a stab of sympathy for Sugar. *How terrible for a chef to have such a problem, and to have people speculating about it.*

"The network worries that people will think Sugar's own cooking caused her condition," Mitzi added. "People are crazy that way."

The chief's skeptical look shifted between Sugar and Mitzi. "Would anyone really try to kill a person for losing weight?"

"No," Sugar insisted.

"Some of the posts have called her a traitor," Mitzi said. "And a couple even said she deserves to die. I delete that kind of thing from the forums when I see it, but I have printed copies."

"I'd like to see them," the chief said. He tapped the pencil against the paper. "Whoever did this must be at the resort, so if we cross-reference the list of rabid fans against the actual guests of the resort that should help us eliminate some of the people." He looked at Mitzi sharply. "Anyone else?"

Mitzi shrugged. "Sometimes the wives and girlfriends of men Sugar flirts with get pretty irate about it."

"That's not fair," Sugar said. "I'm friendly, sure, but I certainly wouldn't be interested in stealing someone else's man. There have been a few teeny-tiny misunderstandings, but nothing worth talking about."

After seeing Sugar flirting with Wolfe, Faith could imagine how a person could get mad about that. Not that Faith was mad. She had no claims on Wolfe. While she reassured herself of this, she turned away from Sugar's protestations of innocence, and her gaze drifted to Mitzi.

As Sugar kept her face turned toward Chief Garris, her assistant stared at Sugar with an intense expression, an expression that looked a lot like rage or maybe even hate. In fact, Mitzi's face and body language suggested she might have a lot of anger toward her boss. Could Sugar's flirting have landed on someone Mitzi cared about? Suddenly Faith wondered if the chief ought to put Mitzi on that list as well.

9

Faith was still watching Mitzi when Chief Garris touched her lightly on the arm to get her attention. "Miss Newberry, may I speak to you in the hall?"

"Of course."

"Should I come too?" Wolfe asked. "Faith is an employee of Castleton Manor."

Sugar reached out and caught his hand. "Oh, I'm sure the chief isn't going to grill her. And I'd like to talk to you about something."

Faith gave Wolfe a reassuring smile. "I'm sure I'll be fine."

"See?" Sugar said brightly, making Faith want to smack her, a feeling that surprised her so much she turned sharply and followed the chief from the room, aware of the eyes on her back as she went. She looked over toward the nurse's station and saw the TV producer was gone.

The chief walked down the hall and turned into a small, empty waiting room. He gestured toward the worn love seat with his pad, and Faith took a seat, smoothing her skirt nervously.

"Please tell me exactly what you saw during both attempts on Sugar's life."

"Both? So you're sure the flowerpot wasn't an accident."

"In light of the poisoning, it seems an unlikely coincidence," he said.

Faith recounted the incident. It didn't take long. "I looked up at the balcony right after the pot fell. I didn't see anything clearly but I thought I saw a flash of movement and possibly something reddish."

"Like red clothing or red hair?" the chief asked.

"I'm not sure. It might have been red hair, but it could just as easily have been a rust-colored hooded jacket or even a hat, I suppose."

"Did you see anyone wearing clothing like that?" he asked.

She thought for a moment. "No one that I noticed. None of the staff uniforms are that color. We had guests coming in all day. I certainly didn't see them all."

"This intern that Miss Worthington's assistant mentioned, Andrew Ashe. You met him?" Faith nodded. "Does he have red hair?"

"No, Andrew Ashe has short, dark hair, nearly black." She suddenly remembered the casual way he was dressed the first time she saw him. "I did see him on the day that the plant fell. He was wearing a rust-color, hooded jacket, but he didn't have the hood up when I saw him."

"But you saw him indoors."

"Yes."

"And the second-floor balcony is outside, where someone might reasonably raise a jacket hood for warmth."

"Yes, though what I saw was so quick that I can't say it was a man in a jacket. It could have been a red-haired man or a woman. It could have been all sorts of things." *Including Mitzi*, Faith thought.

"Fine. Now tell me about what you saw in Miss Worthington's room today."

Faith described the scene in the suite, and the subsequent discovery of the chocolate truffle by Watson. The chief actually smiled at that. "Your cat seems to be quite the detective."

"He has his moments. I picked up the chocolate in a piece of tissue so the dogs wouldn't eat it since chocolate is very bad for dogs. I carried it downstairs in my jacket pocket and managed to remember before it melted. I then put it in the drawer of my desk at the library. I don't know why I didn't simply throw it away, since I had no reason to assume Sugar's collapse was anything criminal. I guess it just seemed strange that the dogs hadn't eaten the chocolate immediately. Dogs normally love sweets."

"I'll send someone by the manor to pick up that piece of chocolate," the chief said. "And I'll refrain from scolding you about moving evidence since you didn't know, but if your cat finds anything else at potential crime scenes, I'd appreciate it if you'd leave it for the police to collect."

"I'm hoping to avoid possible crime scenes in the future," Faith said.

"Good plan. Now, you mentioned an argument between Andrew Ashe and Miss Worthington's assistant. Can you tell me the details of that?"

Faith described it briefly, being sure to mention that Andrew had been the calm one at the beginning of the exchange. The chief took notes without comment, then, when Faith had nothing else to say, he closed his notebook and slipped it back in his jacket pocket. "Call me if anything else odd happens."

"Of course."

She stayed seated for a few moments after the chief had left and relived the falling flowerpot incident over and over, but no matter how much she thought about it, she simply couldn't be sure of what she'd seen. Finally, she got up and walked out to the hall, where she nearly ran into Wolfe.

"I was wondering how long you'd stay in there," he said. "I didn't want to interrupt whatever you were thinking about."

She fiddled with the button on her blazer. "I was trying to remember something helpful about the falling flowerpot, but nothing came to me."

"Maybe you should ask Watson," he said with a teasing smile. "As I remember, he's the sleuth in the family."

Faith laughed. "If he knows anything, he's not talking." She looked back down the hall. "How's Sugar handling the idea that someone tried to poison her?"

He followed her gaze. "She seems to be in denial. I get the feeling that's fairly common for her." Then he turned back to Faith and chuckled. "She's certainly an interesting person."

"Yes, I noticed you two were hitting it off." Somehow her tone wasn't as light as she'd intended, and Wolfe gave her an odd look.

"Is something wrong?" he asked.

She forced a smile. "No. It's definitely been a long, strange day, but some days are like that, I suppose. I should get going. I want to stop and chat with my aunt before heading home. Are you going to be in Lighthouse Bay for a while?"

He nodded. "At least as long as this retreat. I don't want to leave while there is any risk to Miss Worthington's safety, or yours. I'm sure I'll see you at the manor." He gestured down the hall. "May I walk you out?"

Faith agreed and Wolfe turned the conversation to lighter topics by launching into a funny story about his last plane flight and the little boy who'd sat near him in first class and entertained everyone with his cartoon character impressions. Though Faith laughed along with the story, a faint feeling of unease remained with her.

When she left the hospital, she drove to the Candle House Library, sneaking glances at the clock on her dash as she poked along behind slow traffic. Though it was the library's night to stay open late, she'd be lucky to make it before her aunt left for home.

As it was, Eileen was standing on the neat brick patio outside the door of the library, locking up as Faith pulled into a parking spot. Faith's aunt wore a long wool jacket with a hand-knit scarf and matching hat.

Eileen waved as soon as Faith climbed out of the car. "I got your text this afternoon but I thought you weren't coming," she called.

Faith hurried over and gave her aunt a quick hug. "Sorry. I got held up at the hospital."

"Hospital!" Eileen looked Faith over.

"Not for me. I was visiting Sugar Worthington. Did you hear about her?"

"Of course. You know news travels fast around here. Hold on. Let's go inside where we can be comfortable. The cold makes my joints ache, so I'd rather not chat outside." She turned to unlock the door and they headed in. "If you'll set a fire, I'll make us some tea."

"I'm getting to be an old hand at fires," Faith said as she walked over to kneel next to the fireplace. "I'd make a terrific maid on one of those great English estates."

"The ones that scurry in and out without ever being noticed?" Eileen said. "That doesn't sound like much fun."

"Oh, I don't know. The maids knew all about the secret passages. Remember, I told you about the one Watson found at the manor right after I started work. Imagine wandering through the walls of the estate like a mouse. I think that's exciting."

"And dusty. I'll be right back with the tea."

While her aunt was gone, Faith started a small fire since they wouldn't be staying long. When they were finally settled in the comfy chairs with steaming chamomile tea, Faith caught Eileen up on her day. "I was surprised that you didn't show up for the book signing. I should have let you know, but everything was in a bit of a kerfuffle."

"It wasn't a problem. I'd already heard about Sugar's collapse from one of our patrons." Eileen wrapped her long fingers around her mug. "She actually told me just as I was getting ready to leave. Gail and Seth were both here to look after the library while I was out. So I squeezed in some early Christmas shopping instead. I didn't want to waste a good break." Her face turned solemn then. "I am glad to hear Sugar seems to be recovering all right."

"I think she was a little pale under all the makeup she was wearing," Faith said. "But she certainly was flirting up a storm with Wolfe." As Faith said the words, she was glad of the chance to get them off her chest, even if she was embarrassed by the jealousy behind them.

Eileen gave her a mischievous look. "Which you didn't like."

Faith took a deep sip of her tea to hide her discomfort. "It's not for me to like or dislike Sugar's behavior. And Wolfe is free to do whatever he wants, of course. I barely know the man. The most that can be said of us is that eventually we might be friends."

"But you still didn't like it."

"No," she admitted. "I didn't. I think dealing with divas is driving me insane. Nothing else explains it. You know I'm not a jealous person."

"And you probably wouldn't be now if your relationship with Wolfe was a little more settled."

"It's settled," Faith insisted. "He's my boss, sort of, and my friend, I guess."

"That sounds settled."

"It *is*." Faith saw her aunt hide her smile behind her own teacup and found she didn't want to talk about Wolfe and Sugar as much as she'd thought she did.

Her aunt must have decided to have mercy on her, because she changed the subject. "I am sorry the book signing was canceled.

I was looking forward to it. I don't suppose you could get an autographed book for me?"

"I might be able to, but the signing is only postponed. I'll let you know when it's rescheduled. And if it isn't or you can't come, I'll be sure to get you a book. I need to get one for Jane McGee as well."

"Did Jane bribe you with cream puffs?" Eileen asked.

"Something like that." Faith took another sip of her tea.

"So, what is Sugar like? She seems so sweet on her show."

Faith stretched her toes out toward the fire as she thought about her answer. "She is basically sweet, I think, but very used to getting her own way. And I suspect she can be a handful. She certainly loves her little dogs."

Her aunt laughed at that. "That's a point in her favor. But I suppose you have to make allowances for celebrities. I know that's something I would never want to be. What a strange way to live. Your whole life turns into a spectacle."

"I believe it is in Sugar's case. At least if it were up to her producer. They actually wanted to film her in her hospital room."

"That's showbiz, I suppose," Eileen said, shrugging slightly and taking another sip of her tea.

"Well, showbiz is a lot more dangerous than I ever expected." Faith hesitated. She didn't want to gossip about things from work, but Eileen was family. Finally, she added, "The chief came by the hospital. He's looking into people who might want to hurt Sugar. Apparently she has a restraining order against a former protégé. A protégé who is a guest at the resort."

Eileen lowered her cup. "And you've met this protégé?"

"After a fashion." Faith told her aunt about the argument between Mitzi and Andrew. "Though of the two of them, she behaved worse."

"I remember you and Brooke mentioning her at the book club meeting," Eileen said. "She sounds difficult."

Faith nodded. "And there's something about her that bothers me. Well, other than her bossiness. She did offer the chief a clue about Sugar's discussion boards." As soon as she said the words, an idea popped into Faith's head. "Would you mind if I use your computer really quick? I'd like to check out Sugar's forums on the show site while I'm thinking about it. Apparently the fans can be passionate, and I completely forgot to check it out earlier at the manor."

"Sure. You're welcome to use the one in my office." Eileen waved vaguely in that direction. "I'm going to finish this cup of tea and put out the fire."

Faith walked back to the office and settled into Eileen's chair, placing her mug of tea beside the computer. She found the forums easily enough and began reading, fully expecting to discover that Mitzi had overstated the case about "rabid fans," but it didn't take long at all for her to read a number of truly vicious posts, all posted in the last few hours.

The topics included how much Sugar deserved to be in the hospital for falling prey to fad diets and fat-phobic pressures, as well as general hatefulness about Sugar's acting or personality. Faith winced as she thought of how posts like that must hurt if Sugar ever read them. Then she began to spot a number of messages hinting at Sugar behaving badly toward other writers, and Faith saw a few people flatly calling Sugar a thief. Over and over she saw the sentiment that Sugar would "get what she deserved."

Three posters in particular jumped out at Faith because of the intensity of their anger and the way they seemed to be starting so many of the negative discussions. She quickly jotted down their handles: *lovesfood*, *cupcakecassie*, and *spunsugar*. She circled each name on the list and wondered what she should do next. Surely the chief would be checking the boards himself, and she rather doubted he'd appreciate her telling him how to do his job.

"Faith?" her aunt called. "Are you about ready?"

"Coming!" Faith shut down the browser and slipped the list into her blazer pocket, but the mass of viciousness she'd read still spun in her head. Could one of those people be at the cookbook authors' retreat, trying to kill Sugar?

10

The next morning once again dawned unusually warm and bright for October, and Faith left the cottage early to walk through the gardens. Even though most of the flowers were done for the year, the pots of mums and the turning leaves on the trees brought plenty of color, and there was something almost meditative about walking the meandering paths. Faith wondered what it would be like in winter when the crunch under her feet came from snow instead of fallen leaves. She expected the manor gardeners would manage to make the walk beautiful even when the trees were skeletal and the flower beds empty.

As she walked, worry pulled her thoughts reluctantly back to Sugar. Faith wondered if Sugar would be back at the resort soon, and whether that was even wise. She was probably safer at the hospital, especially if the person trying to hurt her was a resort guest.

Ahead on the garden path, Watson chased a dry maple leaf being pushed along by the breeze. He finally pounced on the leaf and chewed it a little before discovering it didn't make a good snack. About the time Faith caught up with him on the path, he suddenly spat out the leaf and arched his back, his fur puffed up. He did a little sideways dance, his gaze directed through the small hedge that blocked their view of the topiary garden.

"What's wrong, Watson?" Before Faith could bend and scoop up the cat, he darted off through the hedge. "Watson! What are you after now?"

With a sigh, she hurried along to the division in the path, following the trail toward the topiary garden. She knew full well there was no point calling the cat. Like all cats, Watson came to her when he wanted unless she made fish part of the invitation. She could simply leave him in the garden to find his own way, but she wanted Watson with her at the library where she imagined she could keep him out of trouble.

She walked around a tall topiary, carefully trimmed to look like a cat, and spotted Cole Venn, who was tangled in leashes as Sugar's dogs, Ginger and Snap, raced around him, barking. Watson, the object of their annoyance, sat on a bench delicately grooming as if he didn't know they were around. Faith hurried over to help unfetter Cole, finally picking one of the dogs up while Cole picked up the other, which made it much easier to untangle the leashes.

"So is dog wrangling a new service of the publicity department?" Faith asked.

Cole laughed. "No, I just like dogs, and normally I'm good with them. We were doing fine until the cat showed up."

"Sorry about that. Watson excels at driving dogs to distraction." She made a face at her cat, who looked at her blankly. "Can you tell which one is Ginger and which one is Snap?"

"Sure. The darker one is Snap." Cole took the dog from Faith's arms. With both dogs close together, she could see that one of the Poms was slightly darker, though they looked identical otherwise. "Plus, Snap is grumpier."

"So his name suits him?"

"A little, but they really are both nice dogs." He looked back toward the manor. "I should get back though. I have a pile of work I'm avoiding by being out here."

Faith picked up Watson and walked with Cole along the path

back toward the house. "At least things should be a little quieter without the TV cameras."

Cole looked at her ruefully. "Don't count on that. I spotted a guy carrying in a Fisher boom as I was coming out, so they must be counting on Sugar being out in the public eye at the resort today."

"What on earth is a Fisher boom?" Faith asked. "It sounds explosive."

He laughed again. "I guess it does. I never thought of it that way. A Fisher boom is a microphone pole that lets the mic operator dangle it way out toward the person speaking without risking being in the shot. It looks a little like a fishing pole."

"How do you know that?" Faith asked.

"I was a film major in college." They had almost reached the main house and Cole gestured toward a small patch of lawn with one of the dogs in his arms. "I'm going to trot the dogs around there for a minute or two before I go in."

"You wouldn't be putting off that pile of work you mentioned?" she teased.

"Maybe a little. It's too beautiful a day to be inside, and I suspect we won't be seeing too many more of these before winter sets in. See you later." He put the dogs down and followed them to the patch of grass. Faith carried Watson up the steps and through the front doors. As always, the first steps into Castleton Manor never failed to impress. She couldn't imagine ever becoming unimpressed with the beautiful marble floors, warmed slightly with equally beautiful handwoven rugs, and the lavish decor. In every corner a plant or floral display brought life to the soaring spaces.

When she reached the library, Faith put Watson down on her desk and got ready for the guests who would be stopping by throughout the day to pump Faith for gossip about Sugar if for no other reason. To her surprise, a young woman in the dark skirt and crisp white blouse that identified much of the resort's help came in and handed Faith a note from Marlene. In brusque tones, it instructed Faith to prepare for the book signing directly after lunch. "I guess Sugar was released from the hospital," Faith said to Watson, who showed all the interest she expected from him, merely blinking at her with sleepy eyes.

She cleared the long library table that would be the perfect location for the signing as it allowed plenty of room for a line to form. She was still arranging books on the table when Mitzi came in, crossing the large library with quick, short strides. She stopped in the middle of the room and looked around, clearly displeased. "You never removed those." She pointed toward the display of cookbooks written by some of the guests of the resort. "This is *Sugar's* signing."

"Yes, I know this is Sugar's signing," Faith said, a thread of impatience in her voice. "But, as I told you, the guests have been told their books would also be on display in the library throughout the retreat, so they cannot be removed."

"Not even during the signing."

"Not even then."

Mitzi frowned. "It can't be helped, I suppose." Then she yelped. "A *cat*. I told you about the cat. This was settled."

"Yes, you did. And I made certain he wasn't here during the time Sugar was scheduled to sign. The reschedule didn't give me a lot of time to prepare."

"Well, he cannot be here now. Sugar will be bringing Ginger and Snap."

"The dogs know Watson. In fact, they were visiting with him about an hour ago." Faith didn't bother to add that Watson was taunting them. She knew it was unlikely that Mitzi would relent about Watson, but she wasn't in the mood to give in too easily to the bossy assistant. Still, in the back of her mind, she wondered if she could possibly rope Cole into cat-sitting during the signing.

Mitzi did stay adamant about removing Watson during the signing, and Faith promised she'd take care of it, though she warned her again that guests might be bringing their pets. Then, to head off whatever other complaints Mitzi might be preparing to unleash, Faith changed the subject. "I'm surprised Sugar feels up to doing the signing today."

"She insisted," Mitzi said, her tone reproachful. "Sugar hates to disappoint her fans. We smuggled her in first thing this morning and she's resting right now, but she'll be ready to join the guests for lunch and then do the book signing."

Faith had handled such events before at other jobs, but Mitzi still went over exactly what she wanted Faith to do. "I'll keep the line of fans in order," she said. "If no one handles the line, it turns into chaos. Your job is to put each book in front of Sugar and open to the flyleaf for her to sign. Don't make her wait for the book. She hates it when she has to wait."

"I can handle that."

Mitzi finally seemed content with Faith's preparations, and she left to discuss Sugar's lunch requirements with the kitchen. Faith spared a sympathetic thought for Brooke, who would probably end up dealing with Mitzi's demands again.

Word of the pending book signing spread, and guests were in and out of the library all morning, checking to see if the rumors were true. Clearly, they were very excited to have the signing back on schedule. Faith managed to squeeze in a quick call to her aunt to let her know about the signing.

Finally, everyone cleared out of the library to gather for lunch in the Banquet Hall and Faith could spare a moment to wonder which of the many Castleton Manor offices were in the basement. She'd been down there before, but she wasn't sure if she remembered one specifically for publicity, which didn't intersect with her library duties very often.

She had just decided to call Brooke and ask her about it when Cole walked through the library door, carrying a fresh poster for the signing. "You're just the man I was hoping to see," Faith said, slipping the cell phone back into her blazer pocket.

Cole grinned as he switched out the poster on the easel. "That's what I like to hear from beautiful women. What can I do for you?"

Faith smiled at Cole's attempt to charm her. "Could you possibly take Watson until the signing is over? Sugar's assistant has made up her mind that he'll be a disruption during the signing. And she's probably right. He does seem to like teasing Sugar's dogs."

Cole scooped up the cat, who purred loudly while Cole rubbed his ears. "It's all in good fun, I'm sure. I can't imagine this guy creating any real problems for anyone."

Then you don't really know Watson, Faith thought, but she merely thanked Cole. "If you'll tell me where your office is, I'll come pick him up after the signing."

"I'm in the basement dungeon with all the other offices," the tall man said.

"I've been there once or twice," Faith said. "I can't imagine a place that is less like a dungeon."

"But it did sound dramatic didn't it?" Cole held up Watson. "I'll bring him up when the book signing is over. I'll need to swap out the poster again anyway."

Faith thanked him again as he headed out with the cat in

his arms. In the intervening quiet, Faith slipped outside to eat her sandwich on one of the benches on the terrace. Soaking up the golden autumn sun, she felt a little sad for the changing of the season. She took a moment to imagine what Christmas at Castleton Manor would be like. She knew they must go all out. With a smile, she thought it was probably a good thing she liked the smell of pine.

Spotting movement through the tall French doors that led to the library, Faith headed back in as the TV crew set up to film the book signing. The bearded man who had spoken with Faith before tossed her a friendly wave, but beyond that they stuck to their work.

After lunch, guests began filing into the library, buzzing with excitement. Mitzi soon followed, quickly bossing the people into a neat line and answering questions about Sugar's health with practiced ease. As annoying as Mitzi could be, Faith had to admit that she seemed to be good at her job.

Then Sugar swept in, carrying her dogs and smiling so wide it made the muscles in Faith's own jaws ache. Her carefully styled mane of curls and perfect makeup couldn't quite conceal Sugar's pallor or the circles under her eyes, but her natural charisma certainly made her seem well.

After waving and blowing kisses to the line of fans, Sugar settled into the chair for the signing and gave each of the little dogs a kiss on top of the head before putting them down on the floor beside her. Faith had left several fine-point markers on the table for Sugar to use, but Sugar slipped a hand into the pocket of her pale pink blazer and pulled out a beautiful gold fountain pen. She saw Faith watching and winked at her. "It's my lucky pen. A gift from an admirer."

Sugar charmed the fans completely, making what seemed like

personal contact with each person as she signed the books. Faith could see why she was such a star. Everything ran smoothly for a while, with fans waiting patiently, exchanging quiet murmurs among them but never taking their eyes off Sugar.

Then all eyes turned toward the library doors as Andrew Ashe stomped in. Faith sneaked a quick look at Sugar and saw her freeze and grow even paler. The young man pushed to the front of the line and began yelling at Sugar. "Why are you telling people I tried to kill you?" he demanded, slamming a fist down onto the pile of cookbooks in front of him. "I did nothing of the sort."

"I never said you did. I would never say anything like that," Sugar said, her voice even sweeter than usual, though slightly shaky. "The police wanted a list of people who were mad at me, and Mitzi gave them one. I didn't even read the list."

"Well, you should have!" he shouted, turning to glare at the crowd as if being fans of Sugar made them guilty of something. He zeroed in on Mitzi and pointed at her. "You've always had it in for me. You were jealous of the attention I got, and now you're getting back at me, aren't you?"

"Hardly," Mitzi said, jutting her chin out defiantly. "You threatened Sugar. You trashed her office. You're a menace."

Faith slid her phone from her pocket to call security, keeping it below the stack of cookbooks so Andrew wouldn't see it. She didn't want to risk getting him more worked up.

"I didn't trash her office!" he roared. "I was looking for evidence of her stealing from *me*."

"Stop saying that word!" Sugar demanded, putting her hands over her ears.

The man paid Sugar no mind, advancing on Mitzi. "You're blowing this all out of proportion to make me the bad guy. I'm the victim!"

Mitzi took a step back from the angry man and looked toward Faith. Her voice shook. "Call security."

As it turned out, Faith didn't have to wait for security, because Chief Garris walked in at exactly that moment, followed closely by Officer Bryan Laddy. "Andrew Ashe?" the chief said.

At the sight of their uniforms, the young man visibly paled and didn't answer. Mitzi spoke up, pointing an accusing finger. "That's him. That's the man who tried to kill Sugar."

Gasps and mutters ran through the waiting fans. Everyone had stepped back to form a circle around the drama of police and possible murderer. "Andrew Ashe, I'm placing you under arrest for the attempted murder of Sugar Worthington." The chief gestured for the young officer to take custody of Andrew.

Andrew held up his hands and took a step back. "I never tried to hurt Sugar. I never would. I just wanted her to admit what she did."

"And when she wouldn't, you settled for revenge. We found the bottle of poison in your room," the chief said calmly.

As Officer Laddy pulled Andrew's arms behind him to attach the cuffs, Andrew kept shouting. "What are you talking about? I don't know anything about poison. I didn't try to hurt anyone."

With the chief on one side and Officer Laddy on the other, Andrew was hauled out of the library, shouting about his innocence the whole way.

11

For a moment, it seemed everyone in the room was frozen, staring at the library doorway. The arrest had seemed almost theatrical—something you expected to see on TV, not in front of you. That's when Faith noticed the film crew. They hadn't been frozen by the arrest. Instead, they panned the crowd, recording the stunned faces.

Faith walked over to the cameraman. "Do you really need to film this?"

The man gaped at her for a moment. "Of course we need to record it. This is ratings gold, lady. Our producer is going to be thrilled when he finds out we got all of it."

"Maybe not." Faith turned at the sound of a familiar voice to see Marlene had come into the library and was now glaring at the cameraman. "You may have recorded it, but you won't be putting it on television if I have anything to say about it, and I believe I do."

The man smirked. "Good luck with that."

Marlene's face reddened and she put her hands on her hips. She leaned closer to the crew. "You will not be putting anything on the air that reflects badly on the resort. I have that in the contract that your producer signed."

"You'd be amazed what the *Sweet & Sassy* lawyers can do with a contract." The cameraman turned away and began fiddling with his camera, clearly marking the end of the conversation.

Faith looked over the faces of the rest of the crew. Only the bearded man she'd spoken with in the past returned her look, glancing toward Marlene and then offering Faith a small smile of sympathy. *Yeah*, she thought, *I deal with her every day.* Still, on this subject, she tended to agree with Marlene. The filming of the arrest seemed ghoulish and inappropriate for a cooking show.

"Everyone? Let's get back to the signing, please." Mitzi stood next to the table, waving. "I'm sure you still want your autographed books." Behind her, Sugar smiled brightly at the line of people, though Faith noticed the smile didn't seem to reach her eyes anymore.

"You handle this," Marlene said, thrusting her finger at Faith. "I need to make some phone calls and track down Elton Fritsch." She stepped to the corner of the library and flipped open her phone while giving death glares to the camera crew, who ignored her with an ease that Faith envied.

Faith hurried back to her post. Remembering her promise to Jane McGee from Snickerdoodles, she opened the book from the closest pile and handed it to Sugar. "Before we get started again, could you autograph this one for a friend of mine? She can't get away from the bakery in town to get it autographed herself."

"Of course," Sugar said graciously. "What's your friend's name?"

Faith told her and Sugar wrote a cute note about how bakers needed to stick together, then handed Jane's book back to Faith. She quickly slipped it off to one side and added a second book for Eileen, which she would get Sugar to sign at the end, if her aunt hadn't arrived by then. Faith smoothly slipped an open book in front of Sugar as the line filed up and the real signing began again.

A couple of people tried to ask Sugar about the arrest, but the pastry chef only smiled brightly at each one who did. "I'm not going to spoil this beautiful day by dwelling on horrible things like that."

Despite smiling and speaking to each person in line, Sugar's mood definitely seemed more subdued. They'd made it through most of the line when Faith looked up from opening a book and saw her aunt smiling at her. "You made it," Faith said.

"I did," Eileen said. "But I may have broken the speed limit a tiny bit." Faith saw her aunt had taken special pains with her appearance, wearing a lovely turquoise sweater in an intricate knitted pattern of cables and lace. Faith was sure Eileen must have made the sweater herself. Her brown hair was up in a neat twist.

"I do like to see people eager for my books," Sugar said, giving Eileen a wink. She looked between Faith and her aunt. "You two friends?"

"This is my aunt, Eileen Piper. She is head librarian at the Candle House Library."

"Oh," Sugar cooed. "I love librarians. It's nice to meet you. Your niece is literally a lifesaver."

"I heard," Eileen said. "I cannot tell you how happy I am to see you looking so well. I hope the rest of your stay in Lighthouse Bay is less eventful."

"I don't know about that. Excitement seems to follow me around lately." Sugar dipped her head to sign the cookbook with a flourish. She handed it over to Eileen and thanked her for coming. Then she dropped her voice to a conspiratorial whisper. "And your speeding secret is safe with me."

"Thank you." Eileen turned to Faith. "I brought Watson a present, some of Midge's cat treats." Midge was not only a terrific vet, but her pet treats made her one of Watson's favorite people.

"Watson is having a playdate with one of our publicity guys because he's a naughty cat who likes stirring up Sugar's dogs."

Sugar waved a well-manicured hand. "You didn't have to put him out for my sake. It's good for Ginger and Snap to get a little sass now and then. Lets them know they're not the center of the universe."

Mitzi stepped up to the table. "I thought it best that the cat wasn't here. I didn't want anything to hold up the signing." She looked pointedly at Eileen, clearly hinting that they were lingering too long.

"That's my cue," Eileen told her, her voice light. "I'll see you later, Faith." She turned and made way for the next person.

Before she could leave the library, Faith called her to the end of the table and handed her the book she'd had autographed for Jane McGee. She asked Eileen if she'd mind dropping it at the bakery when she went back to town.

"I'll be happy to." Her aunt's eyes twinkled as she added, "Who knows? There might be a cream puff with my name on it waiting for me."

Faith watched her aunt head for the library door and spotted Cole in the doorway, holding Watson. She barely stifled a groan. He must have had some duty call him away from keeping the cat occupied. She caught Cole's attention and pointed sharply toward Marlene, who stood near the camera crew, scowling at them. Cole did a mock shiver and mouthed, "Sorry." Apparently he didn't want to be seen with Faith's cat. Faith didn't really blame him. Marlene would probably see it as some kind of goofing off.

Cole started to lean down to put Watson on the floor, but Eileen caught him and took the cat from his arms. Faith watched them talking.

"Faith?" Sugar touched her arm. "Can I have another book?"

"Right." Faith hurriedly opened the next book and laid it before Sugar. "Sorry."

There were only a handful of people left in the line, and they finished quickly. Faith sneaked glances toward her aunt in the doorway several times, and Eileen smiled at her each time. Watson looked completely content in her arms and Faith suspected Eileen was probably stuffing him with cat treats.

When the last person in line had finished gushing over Sugar's reality TV show and left, Sugar sat back in her chair and let her glowing smile slip away for a moment. In its absence, she looked tired.

"Are you feeling all right?" Faith asked quietly. "This must have been a lot so soon after being in the hospital."

To her surprise, the pastry chef didn't attempt to break into her wide smile. Instead she nodded, and the smile she offered Faith was smaller, weaker, and possibly more honest. "I do feel worn out. I think I might head up to my room and take a short nap. Thank you for your help."

"Of course."

While Sugar had been signing, her little dogs had lain quietly in a fluffy pile next to her chair. They hopped up as soon as Sugar scooted backward to stand, and they danced around her feet. Mitzi stepped into Sugar's path and held up her clipboard. "We should go over your speech for tonight. I'm sure you'll want to make some changes in light of everything that's going on."

Sugar frowned at her. "Later. I'm not up to that right now." She stepped around Mitzi and towed her dogs toward the library door. Faith looked toward the door in alarm, hoping the dogs would make it by Watson without incident. Eileen's gaze caught Faith's and her aunt nodded, tightening her grip on Watson slightly, but the cat clearly wasn't in the mood to cause trouble. He simply ignored the dogs.

Snap caught sight of Watson and offered a single yap in his direction, but Sugar shushed him and continued on through the library doors. "Crisis averted," Faith whispered.

"Did you say something to me?" Mitzi asked.

"No, sorry. I was talking to myself."

"Miss Hubert." Marlene's voice was sharp as she stormed across the room. "I want to speak to you about this television crew."

"Of course." Faith noticed the young woman's tone was slightly reticent. Even Mitzi seemed intimidated by Marlene.

Faith heard a soft thump on the table behind her and turned to see Watson rummaging around on the signing table. Apparently Eileen had put him down once the dogs were gone, and he'd made a beeline for trouble. The cat swatted something that flashed gold as it rolled across the table. It was the lucky fountain pen Sugar used for the signing. Faith caught it before it could hit the floor.

The pen looked expensive, and since Sugar had seemed to be fond of it, Faith assumed she wouldn't want to lose it. She looked toward Mitzi, wondering if she should give her the pen, but the young woman was in an intense conversation with Marlene that looked like it might last a while. Faith certainly didn't want to step in the middle of that. She walked out to the gallery to see if she could find Sugar.

She spotted the signature mass of blonde hair near the end of the long gallery hall, partially obscured by a passing group of guests, all clutching their recently signed cookbooks. Faith strode down the gallery toward Sugar, then froze near the statue of Agatha Christie. The group of Sugar fans had passed, and Faith could see that Sugar was talking to Wolfe Jaxon. Actually, what she was doing could be better described as flirting with Wolfe Jaxon. Faith watched as Sugar laughed lightly and rested her hand on Wolfe's arm. He didn't seem to be suffering either, as Faith saw a flash of white teeth as he smiled down at Sugar.

"I'd keep my boyfriend away from Sugar if I were you." Faith jumped at the sound of Mitzi's voice beside her. "She may be talking you up as her hero, but she definitely has her eye on that one."

Faith flushed. "If you mean Wolfe, he isn't my boyfriend. He's my boss." *Sort of,* she added mentally. "I'm certain he can take care of himself. He's free to do whatever he likes."

"Right," Mitzi said.

"He and I aren't involved at all," Faith said firmly.

"Sure. Look, I know how it is with work romances. Still, if that man were interested in me, I'd make sure he didn't get anywhere near Sugar Worthington. I've learned my lesson there."

"What do you mean?" Faith asked.

Mitzi ignored the question. She pointed at the pen in Faith's hand. "Is that Sugar's pen? I do think she'd forget her head if it weren't attached. Let me have it, and I'll give it back to Sugar when I go over her speech with her." She looked pointedly at her boss, laughing. "She looks like she's gotten a second wind without that nap she talked about."

Faith handed the pen over without comment. Mitzi glanced back over at Sugar and Wolfe, then gave Faith a pitying look. "I'll go break them up for you."

Before Faith could assure her that her intervention wasn't necessary, the petite redhead strode off down the gallery. As she watched her go, Faith wondered what had prompted Mitzi's warning. It certainly sounded like she had personal experience. Faith thought again that Mitzi might be one more name on the list of people mad enough at Sugar to wish her dead.

12

Having no real interest in watching Sugar flirt with Wolfe, Faith took a step back toward the library doorway, but then she saw something that stopped her. Police Chief Andy Garris had appeared in the hall. Faith watched him look around, spot Sugar, and stride toward her with the purposeful look of a man on a mission. Curious to see what the chief wanted, Faith started toward them.

A dryly sarcastic voice behind her made her freeze in her tracks. "I have to wonder what my librarian is doing in the gallery when there are still patrons and a film crew in the library with Castleton Manor's priceless collection of books."

Faith turned to face Marlene, determined to keep her next words professional. "Sugar left her pen behind after the signing. I was bringing it to her but managed to hand it off to Mitzi instead."

Marlene raised one eyebrow. "If that's the case, why were you walking in the wrong direction?"

Faith chose to be honest and tilted her head toward the end of the gallery. "I wondered what Chief Garris was doing here."

Now it was Marlene's turn to jump, turning her sharp attention toward the group at the end of the hall. "This retreat is turning into a nightmare. I don't need the guests seeing the police wandering around. I'll go find out what he needs." She whipped her head toward Faith. "You go tend to the library."

Faith didn't appreciate being so summarily dismissed, but since she didn't really have a good reason to stay, she turned and walked back into the library. The TV crew was quickly coiling cables and stowing equipment to move on, now that the signing was over. The tall, slender cameraman who'd remarked on the ratings gold gave Faith a sympathetic smile. "Is that harpy your boss?"

Faith knew he meant Marlene and nodded.

"You have my sympathy," the man said. "And I thought Elton was bad."

"Is Elton difficult?"

The cameraman shrugged. "No more than any producer, really. Temperamental natures seem to come with the profession. He wants to make a good show. We all do."

Faith began clearing the signing table of the last few books. Watson sat exactly in the middle of the table, his head held high like a stumpy-tailed version of some Egyptian statue. "Did you have a nice visit with Cole?" she asked him as she rubbed under his chin. He purred in return, then sprawled on one of the leftover cookbooks. "Sorry, Rumpy, I have to put these away."

The cat gave her a disgruntled look, then hopped to the floor and stalked off across the library. Faith piled up the cookbooks and carried them over to the table that held the main Sugar Worthington display. It was fairly depleted after the signing, but Sugar's face still smiled out at her from the poster. *Wasn't Cole supposed to take that thing?* Faith felt the urge to make a face at the cheerful poster, but she tamped down that bit of childishness.

"Miss Newberry?"

She turned to see Chief Garris had come into the library. His conversation with Sugar hadn't lasted long. "How can I help you?" Faith asked.

"I need to collect that piece of truffle you retrieved from Sugar Worthington's room," he said. "Although we found poison in some of the other truffles in the box, I'd still like to have the one she actually bit into. It's evidence."

"Of course," Faith said. "I put it in my desk drawer to keep my cat away from it."

She led the chief over to the ornate library desk. Along the front edge of the desk, a rack held a selection of vintage cookbooks, the ones not old enough to require special handling yet. The sides of the desk were decorated with relief carving that resembled a large cameo, featuring the face of some distant Jaxon family ancestor. The desk legs were ornately carved as well. Sometimes Faith was amazed that she was allowed to interact with such a beautiful antique, much less to make it her desk.

She pulled open the long drawer under the desk's work surface, expecting to see the tissue-wrapped candy, but instead she only saw the scattered pencils and other office supplies the drawer normally held. She slipped her hand all the way to the back of the drawer, feeling frantically for the soft tissue, but it wasn't there.

"I take it the candy is missing," the chief said after watching her search for a moment.

"Yes."

"Who has access to this desk?"

She winced. "Everyone. I don't really stay tied to the library for every moment once I open in the morning. The rare volumes are under lock and key, so guests have free range of the library. I don't trail around after them even when I'm in here." She gestured around the large space. "There are over ten thousand books here. With all this space, even when I'm in here, someone wouldn't have to wait long for me to have my back to the desk."

"So Andrew Ashe could have retrieved the chocolate."

"In theory, but he'd have no reason to think I had it. He definitely wasn't in the library when I put the candy in this desk. No one was. And I never spoke to Andrew or anyone about it until

I talked to you at the hospital. After that, I forgot all about it."
Suddenly she remembered Wolfe's promise to get the chocolate
delivered to the chief. Apparently he'd forgotten about the chocolate
as well. *Probably too busy flirting with Sugar*, she thought, then
gasped aloud, appalled at her own cattiness.

"Did you think of something?" the chief said, peering closely
at her. "You gasped as if you thought of something."

She felt her cheeks warm. She definitely wasn't going to tell
the chief what she'd been thinking. "No, it wasn't related." She
straightened her shoulders in an attempt to look composed and
professional. "As I was saying, I didn't talk about the piece of
chocolate with anyone in any public spot except at the hospital
with you."

"So Sugar Worthington and Wolfe Jaxon knew about it," he
said, "since they were there when you mentioned the candy. I'll
need to ask them whether either discussed it with anyone."

"It seems unlikely that Wolfe did," Faith said. "If he had, he
would have remembered his promise to deliver the chocolate
to you."

She saw the memory dawn on the chief's face. "That's right.
But that still leaves Miss Worthington and her assistant. I'm not
ready to eliminate Miss Hubert from my suspect pool either, since
she knew Andrew Ashe. She might be trying to protect him."

"Their relationship didn't seem particularly friendly," Faith said.

"That could have been an act. I've learned not to take anything
at face value."

Faith thought Mitzi and Andrew would have to be amazing
actors if the antagonism she'd seen wasn't real. Then she thought
of something else. "I also saw part of the film crew for Sugar's
reality show out in the hall of the hospital. They were too far
away to overhear when I walked into the room, but I imagine

one of them could have gotten closer by the time I mentioned the candy to you."

The chief's eyes narrowed as he processed what Faith had said. "I remember seeing them when I arrived, but that seems less likely than Sugar telling people about it. She certainly has been very casual about her own safety. I cannot seem to convince her of the gravity of this situation."

"That's because Sugar always sees the best in people." This proclamation came from Mitzi, who strode into the library with the determination of a soldier going into battle. "I get paid to be more realistic. So, realistically, what are you doing here at the manor? Don't you have Sugar's attacker in custody? Shouldn't you be shining bright lights in his eyes to get him to talk?"

"You apparently watch too many bad crime dramas," the chief said. "I do have a suspect in custody, but my ability to keep him there would benefit from more evidence, and a more clear-cut motive."

Mitzi crossed her arms over her chest. "Didn't I hear you say you'd found poison in his room? What more evidence could you possibly need? He had the poison in his room! And he considers Sugar to be the thief of his life's work. I don't see the problem here."

"The poison container had no fingerprints on it," the chief said. "Not Ashe's prints nor those of anyone else. And he says he didn't put it there."

"Of course he says that," Mitzi said. "Maybe he was careful about fingerprints. He seems like the methodical type."

"The type who is careful about fingerprints, but careless about leaving the bottle in plain sight? An interesting combination." He looked at Mitzi steadily. "Did you and Miss Worthington discuss the piece of candy that Faith found in the suite?"

Mitzi narrowed her eyes. "No."

"Did you have a conversation about the candy with anyone?"

"Why am I suddenly a suspect?" Mitzi demanded. "You have the culprit in custody. I see no reason to harass me."

The chief raised his eyebrows. "Oh? Do you feel harassed? I'm merely trying to find out how Andrew Ashe could possibly have known about the candy hidden in the desk here. Miss Newberry didn't tell him. I can't imagine Sugar had a conversation with the man. So, if he's the guilty party, how did he get the candy?"

"I don't know," Mitzi said through gritted teeth. "I'm not a detective, and I haven't had any cozy conversations with Andrew. I'd still like to know why you're not off asking him these questions. Isn't that what police officers do, grill suspects until they spill their deep, dark secrets?" Mitzi was crossing the line, as far as Faith was concerned, but the chief didn't take the bait.

The chief smiled grimly. "Sometimes it's helpful to let suspects stew a little before questioning. Not that I need to explain myself to you, Miss Hubert. But I'm also considering every possibility during this investigation. I don't like gaping holes in my investigations, and right now, I'm seeing a big one."

"Well, don't try to plug it with me," Mitzi insisted. "Sugar Worthington is my employer and my friend. I wouldn't do anything to hurt her." She looked sharply at Faith. "Maybe you should look more closely at the person who claims to have hidden the candy in the first place. She probably told half the staff at the house."

Faith startled at the venomous look Mitzi gave her. *Thanks for throwing me under the bus*, she thought. "I didn't tell anyone."

Garris's gaze had never moved from Mitzi, even when she was trying to deflect attention to Faith. "I'm going to go talk with the film crew who were at the hospital that day to see if I can rule them out."

Mitzi jumped on the new topic. "Good idea. Andrew definitely made friends with some of the crew. I saw him having coffee with them several times when Andrew was working with Sugar."

"Do you know the names of the specific crewmembers who were friends with Ashe?" the chief asked.

Mitzi shook her head. "I never paid that much attention, but it's because of that show that Sugar was mentoring Andrew in the first place. She'd never done it before, but the network thought it would be good for the show. They thought it would demonstrate her commitment to giving back."

The chief nodded. "I'll ask around." He bid them both a good day and headed out of the library.

"I can't believe he had the nerve to accuse me," Mitzi grumbled, crossing her arms over her chest.

"He's just being thorough, I'm sure," Faith said soothingly, but inside she agreed with Mitzi. The chief clearly considered Mitzi some kind of suspect. And to be honest, Faith had her own doubts about the assistant's loyalties.

13

Mitzi clearly wasn't in the mood to be soothed and Faith soon gave up. Mitzi finally left the library with her back straight and her hands in fists. Faith returned to her desk, searching the drawer once more in case the truffle magically appeared. She knew it was silly, but the disappearance of the chocolate left her unsettled, as though she'd failed in her civic duty somehow.

At that thought, Faith groaned aloud. She'd completely forgotten to mention to Chief Garris about the posts she'd seen on the online forums. Her gaze turned toward the door of the library. Should she go after him? She knew the chief wasn't likely to overlook checking the online forums, but she still knew she'd feel better if she talked to him.

The library was empty of everyone except Watson, who lay sleeping on the red love seat that faced the fireplace. She stepped out into the gallery and saw a small group of guests standing around the statue of Agatha Christie. As she passed, she could hear them chatting together about the mystery writer's work. Normally Faith would have loved to stop and join in since Christie was one of her favorite authors, but she stuck to her plan and walked on.

When she reached the Great Hall, she could see through the archway that the chief was out in the lobby, talking to the tall cameraman. Faith walked over slowly, not wanting to intrude on the conversation if it was something official, but also not wanting to be away from the library for too long. Luckily the conversation seemed to be winding down and the cameraman nodded at Faith before walking away.

Chief Garris turned to her. "Are you looking for me?"

Now that she had the chief's attention, she wasn't sure how to address the topic. She felt a little silly. The chief must have seen the play of emotions on her face because he said, "It's usually best to speak up. What's on your mind?"

"I know you've probably taken care of this," she said hesitantly. "But if I don't say something it's going to bother me all day."

The chief offered her an encouraging smile. "I promise not to take offense if you tell me something obvious."

"I checked out the online forums for Sugar's television show. Mitzi had mentioned them at the hospital." She hesitated again.

"I remember."

"Of course. There were some pretty vicious remarks posted, but they seemed to come mostly from three people."

He looked mildly interested and pulled out his notebook. "Did you get their names?"

"Not their real names, but their screen names were *lovesfood*, *cupcakecassie*, and *spunsugar*."

"I already have someone checking the forums as well as the printouts of deleted posts that Miss Hubert handed over to one of my officers this morning," he said as he scrawled the names in his notebook. "But I'll make sure they track down these three users in particular." Something in the chief's tone made Faith suspect he was humoring her, but she appreciated the fact that he hadn't made her feel any sillier. "I'm heading back to the station now. I think Ashe has spent enough time contemplating the walls there. I need to ask him some pointed questions. Thank you for your help."

Faith wished him well and watched him disappear through the beautiful arched doors with their elaborate wrought iron embellishments. She turned at the sound of footsteps as someone approached her from the side.

Mitzi had her arms wrapped around herself, her gaze turned toward the same doorway the chief had exited. "I heard your conversation. Thanks for turning his attention away from me."

That hadn't been Faith's intent, but she didn't want to argue the point with her. "Chief Garris is good at his job. The only person who needs to worry is the one who actually poisoned Sugar. Eventually the police will track that person down."

"That's good," Mitzi said, still not turning to look at Faith. "As long as he doesn't do too much damage in the process."

Faith opened her mouth to ask what Mitzi meant by the cryptic remark, but the young woman was already turning away. "I need to go check on Sugar. I think the book signing took more out of her than she'd care to say." She walked away, her boots tapping on the marble floor.

Faith walked back to the library and found that she was able to concentrate now that she'd spoken to the police chief. The library was still empty, so Faith prepared for the group signing scheduled for the next day. That event would involve the five other published cookbook authors. She wouldn't have trouble giving them enough space to avoid any bottlenecks, especially since she didn't expect the kind of line they'd had for Sugar's signing.

She looked around the library, wondering if she should put each author at a separate table or maybe set two to a table. As her gaze swept the room, she was startled to find she wasn't alone.

"Miss Newberry?" A petite woman wearing the dark slacks and white blouse of Castleton Manor staff stood quietly between Faith and the library door, her hands clasped around an envelope and a patient look on her pleasant face. She handed an envelope to Faith. "Message for you."

"Thanks."

The woman nodded silently and hurried out of the library, which surprised Faith. She couldn't imagine not wanting to linger in the gorgeous library, but maybe the woman didn't want to risk Marlene catching her taking a break.

The cream-colored envelope had the expensive feel of linen paper and the envelope flap was embossed with a swirly *C*, which identified it as official Castleton Manor stationery, one of the envelopes every room had for the convenience of guests. She carried it over to her desk and picked up a letter opener to slit the envelope and pull out the folded sheet of paper.

Written with an abundance of swirls and flourishes, which Faith recognized from the book signing, was a single sentence from Sugar. The note asked Faith to meet Sugar out by the stables after dinner. Faith sighed. Technically she'd be off duty then, but she was curious as to why Sugar would want some clandestine meeting out in the cold. But she knew Marlene would consider any guest request a priority, whether Faith was on duty or not. She dropped the envelope onto her desk and went back to work.

The rest of the afternoon was fairly quiet with only a couple of guests dropping by. One wanted to ask about the group book signing after shyly pointing out her own book on French cooking for working moms in the display. The other guest came by wanting a good book to read in the evenings. Faith happily helped each of them.

Since she was going to be meeting Sugar on the grounds, Faith didn't bother heading back to her cottage. Instead, she worked late, replacing all the books she'd used in her presentation and then working on the library catalog. Finally she sat back in her chair and stretched her aching back. She wondered if she'd have time to wander down to the kitchen to see if she could beg Brooke for something to eat.

She found her friend was right in the thick of the dinner

bustle, but Brooke grabbed a salad for Faith and sent her to one of the staff break rooms to eat.

Faith was sorry her friend was in such a rush. She would have liked to talk to her about the last few days. Brooke could be a little overimaginative sometimes, but her unique viewpoint sometimes really helped Faith to sort things out in her mind.

In the empty break room, Faith poked at the salad. It was excellent, with warm grilled chicken, dried cranberries, and delicious spiced pecans on a bed of beautiful fresh greens, but Faith was feeling edgy and distracted. She ate slowly, keeping one eye on the clock as she worked her way through the salad. She was nearly done when Brooke poked her head through the doorway. "Good, you're still here." She hurried over and slipped into the chair across from Faith. "Sorry I couldn't stop before."

"No problem," Faith said. "I'm not taking you away from work now, am I?"

"No, I'm good. I heard about the drama during the book signing. Were you shocked?"

"Definitely." Faith pushed around the last bit of greens.

Brooke looked at her wide-eyed. "You don't think the guy they grabbed did it. I can tell. Spill. What do you know?"

"I don't *know* anything. And he might have done it. I do wonder if there isn't more to this than meets the eye." She glanced up at the clock on the wall. "I hate to run out on you, since I'd love to talk about this, but I'm supposed to meet Sugar. That's why I'm still here."

"Oh? What does she want?"

"She didn't say. I got a note from her asking to meet her out by the stables."

"She wants to go riding? It's going to be dark and cold. They won't let the horses out in this."

"I'm sure she knows that. Maybe she just likes horses. Or she wants privacy. Or she likes being a celebrity with the power to make people come to her no matter where she is."

"We're practically in a castle," Brooke said. "It seems like she could pick someplace that was private *and* warm."

"That would have been nice." Faith laid the fork on the plate. "At any rate, I need to go. I have to run up to the library and collect Watson. I can't leave him in the library all night. It's a good thing Eileen fed him a bunch of snacks during the signing, or he'd be cranky about his delayed dinner. Even so, he's going to be disgruntled when I carry him up to the stable."

"I'm off for the evening and I don't have any plans. Why don't I take Watson to the cottage and wait with him until you get back?"

Faith laughed at Brooke's hopeful expression. "That wouldn't be an attempt to get all the details of this secret meeting, would it?"

"Of course it would," Brooke said. "But I'm also happy to help. Watson and I are pals."

Faith reached into her blazer pocket and handed over the keys to the cottage. "I'll see you as soon as I'm done with Sugar. Thanks for taking care of Watson and thanks for dinner."

The walk to the stable was uphill, but fortunately it was a neatly paved cobblestone path with plenty of lights along the way. Faith could have taken the drive instead, the one the family used generations ago when they'd have taken the horse and carriage into town, but that driveway wound around between the house and the stable. Faith preferred the steep climb over spending any more time outside in the dark than absolutely necessary. With nightfall, a cold wind had swept in that hinted of rain, and Faith definitely wasn't enjoying it. She just hoped Sugar could tell her whatever she needed to say before the rain started and soaked them both. *What had made Sugar want to meet outside in this kind of weather?*

Up ahead she spotted Sugar standing off the path in the grass with her arms wrapped around herself. Sugar stomped her feet a couple of times before hurrying over to meet Faith. "There you are," Sugar said, her tone cranky. "I'm freezing to death out here."

"It *is* cold," Faith agreed. "And getting colder, I think. Why did you want to meet out here anyway? We could have met in the library or in your room."

"Me? You picked the spot. I'm just following the directions in your note. You said you had something to tell me that shouldn't be overheard."

"My note?" Faith echoed as a chill slid up her spine that had nothing to do with the autumn wind. "I didn't write a note. I'm here because of a note from you."

"I didn't write you any notes. Why would I do that? That's just silly."

"What it is," Faith said quietly, "is scary. I didn't send a note and neither did you. So someone else wants us out here in the dark alone. And I can't think of any good reason for that. We need to go back to the manor where there are lots of lights and lots of witnesses, and we need to do it right now."

Faith looked back at the lighted path. Would whoever sent them out there expect to find them on the path? Maybe they'd be better off to go directly down the hill through the grass. They would reach the house more quickly, though they would have to pass through a small stand of trees. Would there be someone waiting? She had to choose. "This way."

Sugar nodded assent and they struck off across the lawn, moving as quickly as Sugar's fancy boots would allow. From the top of the hill at the stable, they heard a sudden clamor, and several horses bolted out of the stable, running at full speed directly through the darkness, directly toward them.

14

With the horses thundering toward them in the darkness, Faith grabbed Sugar's arm and pulled, hoping to get them out of the animals' path, but Sugar's boots definitely weren't made for walking. On the uneven ground, she soon stumbled and fell. Since Faith was still holding Sugar's arm, she fell too. And in a flash, the horses reached them.

Faith wrapped her arms around her head and waited as the horses ran by all around them. The ground trembled under her. She could smell the horses and feel the air movement as they stampeded by. With every passing moment, she expected to feel the pain of being kicked or trampled, but instead, the group of horses parted around Faith and Sugar, doing nothing more than kicking up dirt and dry leaves.

As the horses raced down the hill toward the manor house, Faith tentatively uncovered her head. "Sugar? Are you all right?"

"Scared half to death," Sugar said, her voice high and thin. "But I'm not trampled, so I think I'm doing right well."

Faith scrambled to her feet and helped Sugar up. One of the heels on Sugar's stylish boots was broken, so she wobbled more than usual, but otherwise, they were both disheveled and dirty but unharmed. Faith looked up the hill toward the stable and saw lights come on in the head groom's cottage. More lights shone from the windows in the apartments over the stable where the assistant groomsmen lived. The glow of the windows looked inviting, especially since the cold had finally seeped through her outerwear and she was beginning to shiver.

Within minutes, Faith and Sugar were surrounded by people demanding to know what had happened.

"What were you two ladies doing?" the head groom demanded after he'd sent the other men down the hill after the horses. His white mustache stood out boldly in the darkness, giving him the look of a particularly grumpy walrus. "There's no night riding here, not even for celebrities." He added the last while looking pointedly at Sugar.

"Do I look like I was riding? We weren't riding," Sugar snapped, her normally sweet tone gone. "We were trying to have a conversation when a stampede nearly ran us over. What do you people use for stable doors that all your horses can get out like that?"

"There is nothing wrong with the stable doors. Those horses didn't get out on their own," the groom snapped back, clearly not buying Sugar's story. Faith didn't blame him since it wasn't a night when anyone would just happen to be having a conversation outside near the stables in the dark. He pointed a stubby finger at Sugar. "I'd better get them back uninjured."

Before the argument could escalate further, several security officers from the house showed up, letting everyone know that the police were on their way. After Faith and Sugar gave a brief explanation of what had happened, the rain finally came and Faith found she was having trouble talking through chattering teeth. "Do you think we could continue this conversation indoors?" Faith asked plaintively. "I'm half-frozen and I'd like to avoid going for completely frozen."

For the first time, the head groom looked mildly sympathetic. "You can come up to my cottage. I'll fix you some hot chocolate while we wait for the police."

Though Faith would have preferred to go back to her own cottage, the hot chocolate was wonderful, and the head groom even found wool blankets for them that smelled only faintly like horse. Faith wrapped up in her blanket and sighed. "Thank you." She looked up at the man and smiled. "I didn't get your name. I'm Faith Newberry, the librarian at the manor."

The man's mustache twitched as he smiled. "Samuel Peak. You ladies stay here and warm up. I have to go knock some heads about my horses. The police will be along directly, I'm sure. And we'll find out soon enough who did this. The stable has more security cameras than an airport."

Faith was surprised. "Cameras? Do you have a lot of trouble with theft in the stable?"

"No, but the resort has hundreds of thousands of dollars tied up in those horses, so being especially careful makes sense."

Sugar had been drinking down her hot chocolate, but now she looked up at the groom. "Good! Then the police can put a stop to all this. I'm getting a little tired of almost dying here."

"I have no doubt about that," Faith agreed. "Though it will be a relief to put this evening behind us—and get a hot shower."

But it was a relief they weren't going to have soon. When the police came, they took statements from Faith and Sugar, then asked them to come to the stable office while they checked the videos. Unfortunately, whoever had driven the horses out of their stalls had also disabled the security cameras. The only camera still functioning was the one on a lamp near the long expanse of sloped lawn between the stable and the house. As a result, they were able to see spectacular images of Sugar and Faith nearly dying, but nothing of whoever had tried to kill them.

Looking at the footage of the horses galloping by them made Faith a little queasy. She'd known the horses were close, but in the video Sugar and Faith vanished in the stampede, making it look for a moment as if they'd been trampled.

The police officer reviewing the film, Mick Tobin, apparently caught sight of Faith's face and jumped to his feet to help her into one of the office's straight-back wooden chairs. As she sank weakly onto the seat, Chief Garris and Wolfe came into the office.

"Wolfe!" Sugar said. Faith noticed that although Sugar had looked pale also, she perked up considerably as she smiled at Wolfe.

Wolfe offered Sugar a gracious smile, then turned immediately to Faith. "Are you all right? You don't look well."

Faith felt enormously relieved for Wolfe's strong, reassuring presence. "I just watched myself almost get trampled. It was sobering."

Chief Garris walked over to the monitor where the video was paused. "What did you find?"

"This is the only uncorrupted video," Officer Tobin said. "It doesn't show anything but Miss Newberry and Miss Worthington narrowly avoiding the horses. If the horses were set free with the intention of killing these two ladies, they almost succeeded."

Faith shivered again at the memory and wished she'd kept the blanket the groom had given her. Wolfe slipped off his coat and wrapped it around her. Faith glanced quickly in Sugar's direction, assuming Sugar would do something to draw Wolfe's attention her way, but instead Sugar gave her a small smile and turned her attention back to the terrifying images on the screen.

"Chief Garris, do you still have Andrew Ashe in custody?" Faith asked.

"Yes. Our techs discovered Andrew Ashe was logging into the show forums with the username *lovesfood*, which means he made plenty of angry public remarks and threats. Add that to the poison we found in his room, and we weren't likely to let him go this evening."

"But if he's in custody, he couldn't possibly be behind tonight's attempt," Faith said.

"He couldn't have done it alone, but he could have a partner," Garris said. "Though this does complicate things." He looked between the two women. "I'd like to see the notes you got."

"I left mine in the library," Faith said. "It's on my desk."

"I have mine." Sugar pulled the cream-colored envelope from the pocket of her once-white cashmere jacket.

The chief put on gloves before taking the note. He looked at it, then showed it to Faith. "I assume this isn't your handwriting."

Faith looked closely at the neat, precise lettering. "No, but it also doesn't look like the note I got. The handwriting in the one I received was full of loops and swirls." She looked up at the chief. "I didn't recognize the young woman who delivered my note, but she looked like staff." She described the woman briefly, though she'd not paid particularly close attention at the time.

"My note was delivered by a man," Sugar said with a smile. "He was right cute, with dimples and brown curls and a little bitty bit of a Maine accent. Plus I'm pretty sure he works out based on the way he filled out that white shirt." Everyone in the room turned to stare at her and Sugar shrugged. "I notice men. So sue me."

"So two different delivery people. I'll track them down and find out exactly where they got the notes." Garris turned to look at Wolfe. "I don't suppose either description sounds familiar?"

"No, though I'm not involved with hiring staff beyond a few key positions," Wolfe said. "I expect Marlene Russell can help."

The thought of meeting with Marlene after the day she'd had was more than Faith could handle. "I don't suppose we could do that in the morning? I haven't been home yet, and someone is waiting for me there."

"And I'd like to go back to my room," Sugar added. "I'm beginning to think it was more restful in the noisy hospital where they poked me with needles every time I fell asleep."

Garris looked them over. "That will be fine. The rain has stopped and I can have officers walk with each of you." He turned to Faith. "Would you mind stopping by the library and giving the note to the officer before you head home?"

"That won't be necessary," Wolfe said. "I can collect the note from the desk. Faith should get home and rest."

A sudden burst of gratitude for Wolfe's kindness brought tears to Faith's eyes, making her realize just how spent she felt. She hopped up quickly before anyone noticed her teary eyes. "Thank you. I really would like to go home."

Since he was finished with the video, it was Officer Tobin who walked Faith back to the cottage. He had offered to drive her instead, but she'd insisted that she was well able to make the short walk. She was halfway down the hill from the stable when she began to regret that decision. A nice warm, dry car sounded wonderful, but she forced herself to pick up the pace.

After a few brief attempts to chat, Officer Tobin must have realized from Faith's one-syllable responses that she wasn't up for conversation. The truth was that she had only enough energy to make the walk or to chat, but not both.

When she saw the lighted windows of the gardener's cottage, her knees felt weak from relief. She was almost home. "Thank you for walking with me," she said to the officer. "I'm sorry I wasn't very good company. Do you want to come in for coffee?"

"No thanks," Officer Tobin said. "I'm sure the chief has plenty of chores for me yet. He's going to be grouchy if we have to release Ashe."

"Maybe he'll find Ashe's accomplice quickly." Even as she

spoke, Faith realized that she was far from convinced about Ashe's guilt, especially in light of her near trampling.

The officer gave her a sympathetic look as they reached the front door. "Even if we do have to let Ashe go, you shouldn't see him. The chief will make it plain that being anywhere on the Castleton Manor property will net him an express ticket back to jail. I think you'll be all right."

Faith thanked him, but she wasn't so sure. Whoever had sent the notes to Faith and Sugar seemed to know the resort well, and if someone at the resort was a killer, Faith couldn't feel safe anywhere.

15

Warmth poured from the little cottage, embracing Faith as soon as she opened the door. The pure pleasure of that nearly made her weep. Brooke was in front of her in seconds. "You were gone so long," she said. "Are you all right? You look terrible."

Faith managed a smile. "Thanks."

Brooke waved off the response. "You know what I mean. You're pale and wiped out. What happened? Was the meeting with Sugar that tough?"

"The meeting with Sugar was a ruse. Let me sit, and I'll tell you about it."

Brooke led her to one of the chairs by the fire. The crackle of the flames in the fireplace sounded so welcoming and cozy that Faith found herself blinking back tears again. She was so tired, but as she looked at her friend's face, she knew she wasn't going to get to bed without giving Brooke at least a brief explanation.

"Can I get you something?" Brooke asked. "Coffee or tea?"

Faith shook her head. "I had hot chocolate at the stable." She took a deep breath. "The note I got wasn't from Sugar. She got a note too, supposedly from me. Someone lured us out onto the green in front of the stable."

Brooke's eyes widened. "Why?"

"Apparently for another attempt on Sugar's life, with me thrown in for good measure. Someone turned the horses loose and sent them running down the hill. I thought we were going to be trampled for sure." At that point, Watson leaped into Faith's lap, making her jump and yelp, another signal of how shaken she was. The cat gave her a reproachful look for the noise before settling down in her lap.

"That must have been terrifying," Brooke said. "Did you call the police?"

"The head groom did." She went on to tell Brooke about the cameras and how they were nearly all disabled. "Except the one that shows Sugar and me cowering while the horses almost ran us over. I would very happily never see that footage again."

"I don't blame you. Does the chief have any idea who did it? And why you? Why would whoever is after Sugar go after you as well?"

Faith shrugged. "They probably aren't after me. I was a convenient way to get Sugar out to the stables on a cold night. At any rate, the chief doesn't know who did it. He does know who couldn't have done it. Andrew Ashe, the prime suspect, is still in custody."

"So they have the wrong guy."

"Maybe. The chief thinks maybe Andrew has an accomplice."

Brooke looked at her skeptically. "But you don't think so."

"I don't know what to think. I don't even know if I *can* think. I'm so tired, I'm about ready to have a good cry in the shower and go to bed." She looked at Brooke apologetically. "I hate to throw you out after you looked after Watson and waited up for me, but I'm exhausted."

Brooke hopped up from the chair as if on springs. "Of course you are. What was I thinking? Look, you head on into the shower. I'll put out the fire and go home. I'll lock up after myself so you don't have to worry about it. Then you can go to bed."

Again Faith felt a rush of emotion. She nodded, afraid to say anything and risk crying all over her friend. She stood, feeling as if weights were hanging from her, and set Watson down in the chair. Then she shuffled off toward her bedroom, with the sound of Brooke tending to the fire behind her.

Once she got to her room, she pulled off her clothes and slipped into her robe. The simple task of undressing had exhausted her so she sat on the side of the bed to catch her breath. The bed was so enticing that she was lured into lying down for a second before getting into the shower. She curled up and was deeply asleep in moments.

The cat sat on the bed and batted at the wad of stickiness tangled in his human's hair. Like any cat, he considered his human's grooming to be a reflection on his own fastidious habits. Luckily, his human was normally very clean, despite the bizarre way she stood under running water every day. He shuddered to think about that.

It simply wasn't normal for his human to leave a disgusting thing in her hair. He had to remove it. He knew she would want it out. He scraped at the mass again, and it stuck to his paw for a moment. In alarm, he shook his paw until the wad fell off.

His human swatted at him. "Leave alone, Rumpy," she muttered, still mostly asleep.

He drew back, offended at the ridiculous nickname she insisted on calling him. If she had to call him something other than his name, he would have much preferred "Long Whiskers" or "Flawless Fur," something that actually suited him. He glared at her for a moment, then returned to the problem of that thing in her hair. Whether she used sensible names or not, she was still his human, and that mess had to come out. He grabbed the sticky wad in his teeth and pulled, hard.

"Ow, Watson, cut it out." Faith pushed the cat back away from her and felt several hairs pull loose from her scalp. "Ouch. Leave my hair alone."

After the pain of Watson pulling her hair out, Faith found herself fully awake. The lights were still on in her bedroom, which made the darkness press against the windows. *What time is it?* With a groan, Faith eased herself upright so she could see the clock on the bedside table. It was nearly time to get up.

"Great. I could have used that last ten minutes of sleep, Watson," she said, swiveling on the bed to face the cat. She saw him trying to shake something from his paw. "What have you got there? Was that in my hair?"

She scooted closer to the cat and pulled the sticky mess from his paw. It was some kind of odd fluorescent green tape, the sticky side covered in strands of chestnut-brown hair. "No wonder that hurt coming out," she muttered. But how had she gotten tape in her hair? Logically she knew she must have picked it up in the field when she was trying to avoid being trampled. She'd practically burrowed under the ground to make as small a target for trampling as possible.

As she turned the tape over in her hand, she wondered how something like that had ended up in the field. The odd bright green made it seem unlikely to be something the grooms used on the horses. Was it some kind of clue? "If it is," she said, "it's not much of one." Still she got up and shuffled out to the kitchen to drop the mass into a small plastic bag before finally heading off to get that shower she so desperately needed. If she had time later in the day, she'd walk down to the stable and ask one of the grooms about the tape.

After a shower and breakfast, Faith felt almost human and managed to get to work on time, though she was surprised to walk in on near chaos in the library. Sugar stood next to her book display. The poster behind her seemed to peer over her shoulder, making for a doppelgänger effect that Faith found disquieting.

In front of Sugar, the *Sweet & Sassy* crew swung microphones and pointed cameras. "I was terrified for my life," Sugar said, stretching the words out impossibly long with her drawl. "I love horses, don't get me wrong, but they're a whole different creature when they're galloping out of the pitch darkness to run you over."

Sugar's glance cut toward Faith and her face lit up in a smile. "And here's the hero who saved me—saved us both really. I wouldn't be here if it weren't for Faith." She waved Faith over frantically. "Come on over and let folks see you."

Faith's eyes widened in panic and she held up both hands, mouthing, *no, no, no*. One of the younger crewmen practically shoved her forward where the camera could capture her. At that, Faith made a determined effort to look calm as she walked over to stand by Sugar.

Sugar threw her arm around Faith. "I was sure those horses were going to kill us both, but Faith told me to run. The hill was steep and dark and I fell. Those horses would have trampled me for sure, but Faith shielded me."

Faith turned to gape at Sugar. She certainly didn't remember shielding the other woman. Tripping and falling she remembered. Along with ducking and praying. But shielding was not in her memories from the night before.

She suddenly realized Sugar had stopped talking and clearly expected Faith to speak. Faith swallowed and smiled weakly. "Everything happened so fast."

Sugar chuckled. "Like all heroes, Faith is modest. I'm lucky to be here and lucky to have a chance to finish out *Sweet & Sassy* for all my fans."

Faith stood frozen, terrified that Sugar was going to ask her to speak again. Instead, she heard someone shout, "Cut!" She nearly wobbled with relief. Faith had no interest in a life lived in front of a camera.

"You give me too much credit," she said quietly to Sugar. "I don't think I'm a hero."

Sugar shrugged. "The public loves heroes, but don't worry about it, you won't have to be in the show anymore."

"I'd rather not be in it at all," Faith said. Then she thought of the wad of tape and pulled the plastic bag from her blazer pocket. "I found this in my hair this morning. Did you have any tape on you?"

Sugar looked down at the bright green mess and shook her head. "No. But I did have to brush enough leaves out of my hair to have a bonfire."

"Sugar, I need you over here." Sugar and Faith looked toward the voice, and Faith saw Elton Fritsch staring into a screen before looking up to beckon Sugar toward him. "I might need a little more footage of that speech. Come and look at this."

Sugar looked at Faith and rolled her eyes, but she walked over to the producer. "If you have to do another take, I don't want to be in it," Faith shouted after her. Sugar flapped a hand in her direction, making the gems in her rings sparkle.

Faith leaned against the display table and watched the crew. At first glance, the bustle looked chaotic but as she observed, she saw that each man moved with purpose, clearly knowing exactly what needed to be done at any given time.

"This will stand!" the producer shouted. "We'll wrap up here and head into the breakfast room for some reaction shots with Sugar's fans, then we're on to the salon, so chop-chop, people."

At the producer's announcement, the activity ramped up with the men carefully gathering equipment for the move. As she watched, something caught her eye. The bearded crew member was peeling up bright blue tape from the floor where it had secured a cable. She walked over and the man looked up at her ruefully. "If you're worried about the floor, the tape didn't hurt it. I promise."

Faith shook her head. "I wasn't worried about it." *I probably should have been. Marlene would have a fit.*

The man smiled. "We were warned not to damage anything."

"I don't doubt that." She smiled and held out her hand. "I wanted to introduce myself since we've talked a couple of times. I'm Faith Newberry."

The hand that engulfed Faith's was huge in comparison. Though the crewman was only a few inches taller than Faith, he was a big man with broad shoulders and lots of muscle. "I'm Liam Ahlberg."

"Glad to meet you." She pointed at his hand. "What kind of tape is that?"

He looked down at his hand, clearly surprised by her interest. "Gaffer's tape. We use tons of the stuff."

"Is it always blue?"

"No, it comes in a whole bunch of colors. Sometimes you want to color-code cables so you know what they're supposed to be doing."

Faith held out the plastic bag. "Is this gaffer's tape?"

Liam took the bag from her and opened it, peering in. "Looks like it. Not mine though. I don't ever use that color, but a lot of the guys do. It's handy because you can see it from a distance."

"Yes, I imagine it would be," Faith said. "Were you guys filming up near the stable?"

The man laughed. "No. I can't exactly picture Sugar Worthington schmoozing with a bunch of horses. The farthest we've gotten from the house was in the topiary garden, and even that was just for color. Sugar didn't go out there either."

Both Liam and Faith jumped at the sharp voice near them. "What is it with you guys? Every time I turn around you're flirting with the help." Elton Fritsch stood there, clipboard in hand.

Liam reddened above his beard. "I wasn't flirting. I'm a married man."

"It's my fault again," Faith said. "I needed some help, but I shouldn't have bothered your crew. I apologize." She tried to force sincerity into the words for the sake of the blushing crew member, but she really wanted to yell at the producer for being obnoxious.

The producer swatted the other man on the shoulder lightly with the clipboard. "Fine, but get back to work. We need to be in the breakfast room now."

The other man bobbed his head, then pointedly ignored both the producer and Faith as he returned to pulling up tape and rolling cable. The producer peered at Faith, squinting slightly in a way that suggested he probably needed real glasses instead of the fake ones she'd seen him wearing earlier in the week. "Did you get whatever help you needed?"

"Yes, thank you."

"Next time, maybe simply ask me. I don't mind helping, but I need to stay on schedule."

"I'll keep that in mind," she said quietly.

With a single sharp nod, he turned and walked away to bully some of the other crew members. Faith watched them for a moment. She didn't watch much television, and she had never given much thought to all the people who were involved in putting a show together. Now she was learning the television version of "It takes a village."

Sugar walked up to stand beside Faith, following her gaze toward the grumpy producer. "Don't let Elton bother you. I think he's more bark than bite."

"So you're used to him?" Faith asked.

Sugar laughed. "No. I don't think anyone ever gets used to Elton." She dropped her voice still lower. "Honestly, I'll be glad when this retreat is over, and I never have to deal with Elton Fritsch again."

Faith looked at Sugar in surprise. "Is Elton leaving the show? Hasn't he been the producer all along?"

"He has," Sugar said. "But he's not leaving. I am. Well, actually the show is ending."

"*Sweet & Sassy* was canceled?" Again Faith was surprised. The avid fans at the resort suggested Sugar was popular. Wouldn't the show be also?

"Hardly. *Sweet & Sassy* is the top-rated reality food show in the country, and my agent told me we're doing well in foreign markets too. Plus, my *mysterious* weight loss has this season's ratings skyrocketing."

"Then why is the show ending?"

Sugar sighed. "I'm tired of the grind. I'm tired of living under a microscope. I'm tired of having the whole world think it's appropriate to comment on my body size and every bite I put in my mouth." She smiled tightly. "I'm just plain tired, and I'm putting my foot down. No more reality TV for me."

"That must be a lot of money to walk away from," Faith said.

Sugar's smile softened. "I have plenty of money. And I'll still make plenty from the foreign and syndication rights. It was the network's way of cheaping out. They got out of paying me what my agent demanded by offering me a cut of the residuals since you never know if that will turn into money or not. The network will do anything to keep the bottom line down."

"Clearly there's a lot about reality television that I never knew," Faith said.

"It's a different world," Sugar agreed. "Well, I need to dash up to my room for an aspirin before the workshop on pâte á choux pastry. I'm still sore all over from last night."

"I'm a little achy myself," Faith admitted. "I didn't know you were giving a workshop this morning."

Sugar laughed. "I'm not giving it. I'm sitting in."

"Wouldn't you know all about how to make cream puff pastry?"

"Of course, but the network thought it would make me look humble and teachable if I sat in on some of the workshops. It's all about image, darling . . . for a few more days anyway." Sugar turned and started to walk away, then stopped and whispered to Faith. "You want to be sure to catch my farewell speech on the last day. I'm going to drop a bombshell and let all my fans know about my medical condition. I'm tired of having them speculate about my weight, and I'm tired of lying to the people who have always supported me. As soon as I finish this gig, I'm never going to be fake to my fans again."

At that, Sugar turned again and hurried out of the library. Faith was left with her mind whirling. She wondered who else

Sugar had confided in about her planned announcement. Would someone want to kill her before that particular publicity bomb could blow up?

Then she turned back to watch the producer rushing the last of the crew from the library. Even if they didn't know about Sugar's plans, every member of the crew was looking at the end of this particular job. Would any of them be angry enough about that to kill the goose for no longer laying golden eggs? Suddenly Andrew Ashe seemed even less like a sure thing, and Faith felt surrounded by danger.

16

With the library finally empty, Faith began to set up for the after-lunch book signing with the authors from the retreat. She assumed the signing would be considerably less eventful than Sugar's. At least she hoped it would be.

She borrowed the easel from Sugar's display, tucking the poster of Sugar in among the books. Not surprisingly, no one from publicity showed up with piles of materials to advertise the *lesser* signing, so Faith had simply printed up some of her own. She propped the poster she'd made for the new signing on the easel and set it up near the library door. The signing was listed in the retreat schedule and would be announced at lunch, so Faith hoped the authors would have plenty of people show up.

Her attention was drawn away from her musings as a group of three guests came in, buzzing with questions about the poster. One of the three, a young woman with eager eyes and short bobbed hair, asked, "Are any of the authors famous?"

"I believe the author of the Cajun cookbook has an active following online," Faith said, resisting the urge to frown. As a librarian, she was annoyed with the whole fascination with celebrity. Surely a book's value was in its contents, not the fame of the author. She was used to the guests at the resort being avid readers, so she'd read all the cookbooks featured, assuming people would want to discuss the recipes.

The three women hurried over to the cookbook display to flip over books and look at the photos of the authors on the back.

Faith sighed and followed them, in case there were any questions about what was inside.

The rest of her morning seemed to follow the same course. The guests dropping in were definitely more curious about the authors than the books for the upcoming signing. Faith pointed out a few of her favorite recipes from the books and did at least get people flipping a few pages.

The flow of visitors dried up over the lunch hour, and Faith managed to sit and catch her breath. She was starting to wish she'd brought something to eat when a familiar face peeked around the library doorway.

"Brooke!" Faith hopped up, happy to see her friend. "How did you sneak out of the kitchen?"

"I bribed the line cooks to cover for me," Brooke said. She carried over a foam box and handed it to Faith. "I was worried that you might skip lunch again, and you need to take care of yourself."

Faith peeked into the box and was delighted to find more of the fantastic salad she'd had for dinner the night before. "I noticed that you seemed to like that one," Brooke said.

"I can't imagine not liking anything that comes out of the kitchen downstairs. I want to thank you again for looking after Watson last night. You must have worn him out. He didn't even follow me to work today."

"We did have some rousing games of chase the paper ball," Brooke said. "Once he got over the indignity of it, he enjoyed it as much as I did."

"That's probably why he was so fascinated by the tape in my hair this morning," Faith said. "You taught him to chase anything wadded up."

Brooke held up her hands. "I plead guilty. But what's this about tape in your hair? That sounds painful to remove."

"Especially when you have a cat for a hairdresser." Faith put the salad container down on her desk and took out the plastic bag from her pocket. "This was stuck in my hair. I must have picked it up in the field when I tripped and fell last night. One of the television crew said it was gaffer's tape."

"Gaffer's tape?" Brooke echoed. "They must be filming *Sweet & Sassy* all over the property."

Faith shook her head. "According to Liam Ahlberg, the guy I talked with, they hadn't done any filming near the stable. Apparently they never went farther than the topiary garden."

"Maybe the ball of tape blew away? The wind off the water has been blustery in the late afternoon."

"But then it would blow the tape farther away from the stable, not toward it." Faith slipped the bag into her pocket.

"Maybe one of the crew likes horses and went up there on a break," Brooke said. "If they use a lot of that stuff, he could have had it stuck to him and it fell off."

"Maybe," Faith agreed. "Or maybe it fell off when he walked up to turn the horses loose and try to kill us."

"Why would the film crew want to kill you or Sugar? Is she that hard to deal with?"

"She doesn't seem to be, but she's planning to leave the show. Maybe someone is mad about losing a job. I imagine someone like Elton Fritsch makes good money producing a show like this."

"That seems a tiny bit far-fetched. And doesn't the chief already have a suspect? Someone who had poison in his room?"

"Someone who couldn't possibly have let the horses loose."

Brooke gave her a worried frown. "I wish I had an answer. I really don't like how you've gotten caught up in this. I think maybe you should avoid being out alone or alone with Sugar for the rest of this retreat."

"I'll think about it." Faith turned to gesture toward her desk. "For now, I need to gobble down the fantastic lunch you brought me before the guests begin arriving for the book signing."

"Oh, right, I saw the poster. Well, good luck with it. I need to get back to the kitchen. But promise you'll be careful."

"Promise."

Once Brooke was gone, Faith had time to eat the salad and finish preparing for the signing, piling up books on the tables and laying out markers, before anyone else wandered into the library.

The five authors for the signing came in together, clearly wired with excitement about signing their books. Faith sat them down with two authors at one table and three at another. "Since there are five of you and one of me, I'm afraid I won't be able to open books for you the way I did for Sugar."

"That's all right, miss," the wizened Cajun cook said, flashing bright white teeth at her. "I think we can manage to open our books just fine. We're happy for the chance to share them with people."

"Great. I'll herd people into the lines." She glanced toward the door and saw people already wandering in. "In fact, I'll get started right now. Good luck."

The signing went well and Faith was glad to see that all the authors seemed to have fans of their cooking. It was nice to have an event go so smoothly. No one barged in to make accusations. No one got arrested. Faith managed a hopeful thought that perhaps the really scary part of this retreat was finally over. She really should have known better.

As dusk was settling in around Castleton Manor, Faith scooped up the last pile of misplaced books to reshelve. She walked by the French doors leading to the terrace and caught a flash of movement from the corner of her eye. Looking down, she spotted Watson, his nose practically pressed to the window. She shifted the load of books to one arm and opened the door. "What have you been up to all day?"

Watson poked his nose in and sniffed.

"Come on. Hurry up. I don't want to let in any late-season moths," Faith scolded. Watson stepped daintily into the library. "And don't disappear on me."

The cat obligingly followed her from shelf to shelf as she put away the misplaced books. Finally she scooped him up and gave him a gentle hug. "Time to head home. It's been a good day."

The short time she'd taken putting away books meant dusk had given way to dark, so Faith decided to carry Watson as far as he was willing to allow. She didn't want him taking off on one of his adventures. She would rather he came into the cottage for the night. The estate property contained abundant wildlife, and Faith suspected some of the night creatures wouldn't be friendly to nosy little cats.

Most of the paths through the gardens were well lit for the security of any guests who liked walking at night. With the distinct nip in the air, Faith doubted many people were out walking, but she appreciated the lights. She tried to sort out her thoughts about the attacks on Sugar. Was Andrew Ashe really the villain? And if so, who was his accomplice? Could it be someone connected with the filming of the television show or maybe Sugar's pushy assistant, Mitzi?

Her musings were broken when Watson began to squirm in her arms. They were close to the cottage, so Faith assumed he was eager to run ahead where he could demand she hurry up and attend to his dinner. "Yes, starving one," she said as she put Watson down on the path. "We'll be eating in a few minutes."

To her surprise, Watson didn't dash ahead to the front door where a light made a small puddle in the darkness. Instead, he darted off the path and ran toward the far corner of the cottage where a low fence set off part of the flowerbeds. "If there's a skunk over there, leave it alone," Faith yelled after the cat. She stood squinting into the darkness for a moment. "I'm going on. Don't blame me if I get to eat dinner first." She thought the word "dinner" would bring the little cat back, but it didn't work.

Faith sighed and continued toward the door of the cottage. She'd barely gone three steps when Watson started yowling, the same rolling alarm sound he'd made on the terrace before the flowerpot nearly hit Sugar. "Watson? What is it?"

The cat continued to yowl. As Faith stepped away from the clearly lit path and into the shadows, she pulled her keys out of her pocket and turned on the tiny flashlight that hung from the key chain. The light barely nudged the darkness at the corner of the cottage but she felt better for having it.

The cat's yowling stopped as suddenly as it had begun. "Watson?" Faith called again. The silence was nearly as unnerving as the noise had been. Faith had to force one foot in front of the other when all her instincts were screaming at her to turn around and run for the front door of the cottage.

A rustling of small branches preceded a burst of motion, making Faith shriek and drop her keys, just before Watson flashed by her. "Oh great, Rumpy. You're going to be the death of me yet."

She bent to gather up her keys, then noticed a glint of reflection from the flashlight beam. She turned toward the shrubs at the corner of the house and gasped. The light was reflecting from the pale skin of someone's hand, motionless against the ground.

Faith snatched up the flashlight and moved closer, quickly recognizing the motionless face of the prone figure, partially obscured by the shrubs. It was Cole Venn. She knelt beside him and reached a shaking hand out to touch his hand, terrified of finding it stiff and cold. But the flesh was warm to her touch and she found a strong pulse when her fingers pressed into his wrist.

"Cole?" she said, shining the light on his face. His eyes were closed and much of his face was obscured by blood. He showed no response to her voice. She fumbled her cell from her pocket and quickly called for help.

The operator cautioned her not to move him since he was clearly breathing. "You don't want to injure him more."

"Is there anything I can do to help him while we wait for the ambulance?" she asked.

"Are you in a safe location?" the operator asked. "If not, it might be best if you waited in a safer, well-lighted area. You can direct the ambulance crew."

"I don't want to leave him."

"Well, in that case, a blanket would be good. Cold and shock are probably the biggest dangers he faces."

"Right, I'll go get one."

"I can stay on the line," the operator said.

"Thank you," Faith tilted the phone away from her mouth and patted Cole gently on the shoulder. "I'm running inside to get you a blanket." Carrying the phone in one hand, she stood and hurried to the door as quickly as the dark night would allow and found Watson seated on the doorstep. Her hands shook from a combination of shock and chill as she unlocked the front door. The cat darted into the house ahead of her, but she barely noticed.

Faith hurried to the spare bedroom, raised the blinds, and turned on all the lights to allow light to spill outside, hoping it would make tending to Cole easier. Then she grabbed the heavy wool afghan from the foot of the guest bed. It was one her aunt had knitted for her, but she was sure Eileen would approve of it being used to help an injured man.

She heard a sound from her phone and raised it to her ear. The operator asked if she was all right, and Faith told her she was taking the blanket to Cole.

By the time she had spread the blanket over Cole's still body, she could hear the faint sound of sirens approaching. "Help is coming," she said aloud, patting Cole gently through the thick afghan. She checked his pulse again and found it still strong. "Hang in there."

The emergency crew was brisk and efficient when they arrived, herding Faith gently out of the way so they could evaluate Cole. Faith stood with her arms wrapped tightly around herself, praying silently for the young publicity assistant while questions whirled in her head. What was Cole doing out at her cottage? And why would anyone attack him? It had to be an attack. He hadn't partially concealed himself under the bush.

Faith turned sharply at the sound of another car on the drive to her house, then another and another. The police had arrived, and they all had questions when they got to the scene. The medical crew waved them away to focus on preparing Cole for travel to the hospital.

To Faith's surprise, Chief Garris walked up to her. "This is your cottage?"

"It's part of the Castleton Estate," Faith said, "but it's where I'm staying."

"Do you know why Cole Venn would come out here to see you?" the chief asked.

"No. I wasn't expecting him." They both fell silent as the emergency techs finished strapping Cole to the stretcher and loaded him into the ambulance. The ambulance finally rumbled away, lights flashing. "Could his head injury possibly have been an accident? It's dark out. I don't suppose he could have tripped and hit his head."

"It doesn't look like it," the chief said. "We can't find anything near him that he could have hit. I'm fairly certain he was attacked."

"But why Cole?" Faith asked. "Do you think it has anything to do with Sugar?"

"It would be a weird coincidence if it didn't, and I don't like coincidences." He put his hands on his hips and stared off into the darkness. "You know another coincidence that I don't much like? This guy was attacked after I released Andrew Ashe."

"Did you let him go because of last night?" Faith asked.

"That was the leverage his lawyer used to force our hand," the chief said. "He couldn't have been involved in letting the horses go unless he had an accomplice. Though it's possible that silencing his accomplice is the first thing he did after getting out."

"You think Cole was Andrew's accomplice? But why? Cole works for Castleton Manor, not Sugar."

"Ashe was attending the cookbook authors' retreat. He might have come into contact with Venn and paid him for his help."

Faith couldn't picture the cheerful publicity assistant setting horses loose to trample her and Sugar to death. It simply didn't fit. Then she had a thought.

The chief looked at her intently. "What?"

"This morning I found gaffer's tape stuck to my hair. I must have picked it up in the field last night." She reached into her jacket pocket and pulled out the bag with the wad of tape.

The chief looked over the bag. "How do you know this is gaffer's tape?"

"I saw one of the *Sweet & Sassy* crew using tape like this in a different color, a man named Liam Ahlberg. I asked him about it. He said that shade of green is popular because it can be seen from a distance."

"So someone from the crew could be involved."

"Maybe." Faith looked down at the toes of her shoes, deeply shadowed by the darkness around them. Finally, she made a decision. "Cole told me he was a film major in college. He recognized a Fisher boom. It does seem an odd coincidence that he has a film background, and then I find gaffer's tape at one attack, and then Cole ends up the victim of another attack. What if Cole has ties to the crew that we don't know about, ties that made him suspect one of them? If he confronted someone, that person, not Ashe, might have needed to silence him."

The chief's expression turned skeptical. "So you think there's some kind of film crew conspiracy and Andrew might not be involved in this at all? I'm hesitant to consider that since we found the poison in his room. I'm not about to give up on Andrew and an accomplice, who might be Cole."

"If you're right, and Cole was somehow involved, that still doesn't mean Andrew has to be guilty. Cole is staff. He wouldn't have had much trouble getting into Ashe's room to plant evidence."

"So do you see Cole as the culprit or an innocent man? And what was he doing at your cottage?" the chief asked. "Trying to finish the job he started in the field?"

"Or trying to come clean about his part in it. Or trying to warn me about something he'd discovered if he isn't involved at all," Faith said. "I don't know. I feel like I'm looking at a jigsaw puzzle dumped on a floor and trying to figure out what picture it makes. I can tell the parts go together but I have no idea how."

The chief chuckled dryly. "Welcome to my world. Still, I don't like the coincidence of Ashe's release and Venn's attack. I think I'll check to see where Ashe went after his lawyer got him out."

"Do you ever get to go home?" Faith asked, suddenly feeling very tired.

"I was home, but with a high-profile case like this, I need to answer every related incident. It would be nice if we could slow down on the incidents for one night, though."

"I agree with that," Faith said. "Will you let me know when you hear about Cole? I really can't picture him wanting to hurt me, but I would like to know why he was out here at my cottage."

"That's a question I'd like answered too."

"Speaking of questions," Faith said. "I assume the note I got wasn't really in Sugar's handwriting."

The chief shook his head. "It wasn't even a particularly good forgery, though it wouldn't have to be. You hadn't seen many examples of her writing." He smiled slightly as Faith stifled a yawn. "You should get inside. If you don't mind, I'll send an officer in first to check out your cottage, to be sure it's safe."

Faith's eyes widened. "I was already in there. You think the attacker might be inside?"

"Probably not since you've already been in, but I want to be certain." He called over Officer Laddy and sent him in to check out the cottage. Faith waited nervously until the officer came back out to give the all clear. The chief turned to Faith. "I'll wait out here while you go in. Engage all your locks and don't wander around outside tonight, okay?"

"That's one promise I have no trouble making." Faith slipped into the cottage and locked the door behind her. Normally she found the snap of the lock sliding into place reassuring, but tonight she hoped it would be enough to keep her from harm.

17

The next morning, Faith left for work early. She had tossed and turned half the night trying to make the puzzle pieces of the last few days fit together in a logical way. She was missing too many key bits. But today she planned to talk to someone who might be able to fill in some blanks. Not that Faith expected the conversation to be pleasant.

As Faith headed down to the basement, she stuck her head in at the kitchen to say hi to Brooke. The smell of fresh baked goods met her and her friend rushed over. "I heard there were emergency vehicles at your cottage last night! I tried to call you, but you didn't answer. I was about to panic."

"You tried my cell?" Faith pulled her phone out of her pocket and saw it was dead. She hadn't charged it. Normally she was quite methodical about keeping the phone charged. With a sigh, she slipped it back in her pocket. "I must have been more stressed last night than I thought. The sirens weren't for me. One of the publicity department staff was attacked near the cottage."

"Oh, how horrible," Brooke breathed. "I don't know anyone in publicity. Was this a friend of yours?"

"I barely knew him, but he was friendly."

Brooke's eyes widened. "Was? Did he die?"

"No, sorry, I'm sure he's still friendly, if he's feeling well enough. As far as I know he didn't die, though he was unconscious when they took him to the hospital. Chief Garris promised to let me know about him today."

"I hope he'll be all right," Brooke said softly. "Did you come by for breakfast? I made some muffins."

"No, I ate." Faith sighed. "I'm actually on my way to Marlene's office."

Brooke wrinkled her nose. "You have my sympathy." She dropped her voice to a whisper. "Her office is entirely too close to the kitchen, if you ask me. We're often her first stop on the nag trail."

Faith chuckled. "I'll be doing the stopping today. I need to go see if she's in. I'll talk to you later."

"Good luck."

The delicious kitchen scents followed Faith down the hall, but now they mixed with the waxy scent of wood polish. The look of the basement was totally different from the upstairs rooms of Castleton Manor but not without charm. Space was tighter, though far from claustrophobic, and the walls of the corridors were mostly plain with well-worn wood floors. The office spaces had once been servant quarters when Castleton Manor was a private residence.

Faith found the door to Marlene's large office open, so she stuck her head in and rapped on the door molding. Marlene was half sitting on the corner of her desk, leafing through papers on a clipboard. "Good morning," Faith said.

The look Marlene turned in her direction suggested the other woman found the morning anything but good. "I heard you brought police attention to us again yesterday."

"Actually, I didn't," Faith said. "I merely called for help when I found a member of the publicity staff unconscious. My main concern was his medical care."

Marlene narrowed her eyes, then turned her attention dismissively back to the papers on her clipboard. "Of course."

"I assume you know Cole Venn?" Faith asked.

"Naturally."

"I'm curious about his background. He said he had a film degree."

Marlene appeared to be barely listening, still not looking up from her papers.

"I wonder if he has any connections to the *Sweet & Sassy* crew," Faith said. "Or to Sugar? It seems odd that he would happen to be attacked during a retreat where there have been several attempts on our guest speaker's life."

Marlene looked up sharply, jutting her head toward Faith. "I expect you to keep quiet about the unfortunate incident last night. The police will handle it. Our responsibility is to the resort and to its reputation, and that means not spreading gossip about attacks or anything else unpleasant. Do you understand?"

"I have no interest in hurting the resort's reputation, but considering I was nearly injured twice this week, I am interested in finding out who is behind this. What surprises me is that you are not."

"I'm only interested in having the unpleasantness stop." Marlene turned her attention downward again. "Personally, I think you're a magnet for trouble and I would go looking for a more suitable librarian, but it isn't my decision to make."

This surprised Faith. She wasn't shocked that Marlene didn't like her. That had been obvious from the beginning. But she was surprised to hear that Marlene wasn't the one making hiring and firing decisions.

Marlene looked up again. "You're still here?"

"I'd still like to know more about Cole Venn."

Marlene sighed dramatically. "I'm glad we're nearly at the end of this cookbook authors' retreat. The guests will be leaving soon, though we're stuck with a few more days of the film crew and Miss Worthington since the network paid for it. Still, this should all be over soon."

Faith was so surprised by Marlene's words that she was temporarily distracted from her reason for coming to the office. "Why would Sugar and the crew stay longer than the rest of the guests?"

Marlene snorted. "Apparently they need the extra days to 'make the magic.'" She pointed a long, thin finger at Faith. "I want these last days to be quiet and uneventful. That means that all the staff keep quiet about anything unsavory. We don't want our guests leaving with the wrong idea about this resort. You're part of the staff so I expect you to follow my directives."

"But there must be some connection between Sugar and Cole Venn."

"You need to pay more attention to your job and less attention to poking into the affairs of our guests. If you want a mystery, read a book. While you're at work, I expect you to work, not gossip, not ask questions, and not investigate. Just work."

Faith closed her mouth against the comments that wanted to come out. Clearly Marlene wasn't going to be any help in providing more information about Cole and any connection he might have with Sugar or the film crew.

"Do you understand me?" Marlene asked.

"Perfectly."

"Then I believe we're done here. Close the door on your way out. Clearly an open door is too much of an invitation for people to wander in."

Faith stepped out of the doorway and pulled the door shut as sharply as she dared, wishing she could give in to her urge to slam it and then kick it a few times. Marlene was easily the most abrasive person Faith had ever met. As she stood in the hall, Faith considered her next step. She could ask Mitzi or Sugar about Cole, but if either of them didn't like the question, it could get back to Marlene. The assistant resort manager might not be able to fire Faith, but she could definitely make her life miserable.

Faith decided to ask Liam about Cole. The burly crew member didn't seem to mind chatting. Plus, he was unlikely to carry tales back to Marlene. The trick would be catching him when Elton Fritsch wasn't around. The producer drove the crew hard and was as unlikely to abide "loafing" as Marlene. Then Faith had an idea.

Hurrying down the hall to the kitchen, Faith poked her head in and caught Brooke's attention. Her friend grinned at her. "You survived the lion's jaws."

"Barely. Can I ask you something?"

Brooke wiped her hands on her apron as she walked over to join Faith. "Sure, what about?"

"Does the film crew eat down here? And if they do, do they eat with the producer?"

"Yes and no. Yes, the regular crew eats in the staff break room sometimes, but the producer eats upstairs. Marlene didn't want any of them eating with the guests, but apparently the producer threw a temper tantrum about it that even intimidated Marlene, and you know that's not easy."

"I've seen some of his temper," Faith said. "It's impressive."

"Maybe, but I think Marlene could take him in a cage match."

Faith laughed at the image that called up in her head. "Do you know about what time they come downstairs? I really need to talk to one of the guys without the producer or Marlene knowing about it."

"You know how I love all this secret spy stuff," Brooke said. "I could call you when they come down." Then she laughed. "Oh, right, your phone is dead."

"I have a charger in the library. I'll plug in the phone as soon as I get upstairs so I should be able to get your call. The guy I'm interested in talking with is burly with a beard."

Brooke's face brightened. "Liam! He's nice. He showed me pictures of his little girl. She's barely a year old and very cute. No problem. I'll call as soon as I see him." Then her smile slipped away. "I can't promise Marlene won't catch you though. She likes to make surprise visits to the staff areas just to be sure we're not slacking off."

"That would be bad. I definitely don't need two run-ins with her in one day."

"I'll let Liam eat, then call you and you can meet him in the baker's pantry. Marlene never goes in there. It'll be very clandestine."

"You'd make an excellent spy," Faith said. "That sounds like a good idea. I hope Liam will actually have some answers after I've gone to all this trouble. I have to do *something*. With Cole attacked on my doorstep, I can't ignore this."

"As long as looking for answers doesn't get you into more trouble," Brooke said hesitantly.

"It won't." Faith gave her friend a reassuring smile and hoped her own words were true.

18

The morning moved like iced molasses as Faith helped guests find specific recipes while they still had access to the library's extensive cookbook collection. Normally she loved that kind of work, connecting people and books, but it was hard to lose herself in her job with everything that had happened during the past few days. She just wanted lunchtime to arrive so she could get a few questions answered.

"Is it true that someone was attacked in the library last night?" one guest asked her in a loud whisper.

The shocking question jerked Faith out of her thoughts. "No, of course not. The library is perfectly safe. Where did you hear that?"

The woman looked slightly abashed. "Someone said it at breakfast." She smiled weakly. "I thought they were wrong, but I figured I'd ask in case someone tried to hurt Sugar Worthington again. That would be awful."

"Sugar is just fine, I'm sure. Didn't you see her at breakfast this morning?"

"I saw her. She looks tired, I think. And that dreadful woman who follows her around looked entirely too full of herself. I bet they find out she's the one who tried to drop that flowerpot on Sugar and attacked her in the library."

"No one attacked anyone in the library."

"Oh right." The woman reddened. "Well, I bet she would have."

"What makes you think that?" Faith asked, hoping to reflect her genuine curiousity.

"That redhead is too busy trying to look like she hangs on every word Sugar says, but she's as fake as diet soda. I can tell. I have a sister-in-law who is just like that, all sweet in your face and sticking knives in your back. I can spot the type."

Faith suddenly had the horrified realization that she was gossiping with a guest. Not only would Marlene blow a fuse, she'd have every right to do it. When Faith didn't speak for a moment, the guest looked uncomfortable and started babbling. "Anyway, I'm glad no one was really hurt here in the library. It's a beautiful place. And besides, libraries should be safe places, you know?"

Faith wondered when the rumor mill had changed "librarian's cottage" into "library," but she didn't intend to enlighten the woman about the real location of the attack. "I assure you, you're perfectly safe anywhere in the manor."

"Good. I've had a wonderful time, and I've learned so much. I don't have a cookbook ready to publish yet, but I feel like I could manage one now. I want to do some French-Mexican fusion dishes."

Faith blinked as she tried to imagine what that would be like. "That's an interesting combination."

"My mom was from France, and my dad was Mexican. They met here in the United States. Mom always tried to cook the food Dad grew up with, but somehow it always turned a bit French in the preparation." She shrugged. "So to me, that's simply home cooking."

"I'd love to try some," Faith said. "It sounds unique."

"I could give you my mom's enchilada recipe." The woman began rooting through her purse and pulled out a small notebook. "It uses brie." She looked around the room. "Do you have a copier?"

Faith tried to picture brie in enchiladas, then inwardly she gave a mental shrug. *It might be good.* She led the woman to a mostly hidden corner behind the spiral stairs where her printer and scanner were set up so they didn't look so jarring in the beautiful library.

The rest of the morning stayed busy, but the crowd thinned as lunch approached and finally Faith stood alone in the big room. As she walked around straightening and reshelving books, she unplugged her phone and slipped it into her pocket so she'd be ready the moment Brooke called.

She didn't have long to wait.

"The eagle has landed," Brooke whispered into the phone, then giggled.

"An eagle?" Faith said.

"You're right," Brooke said. "More like a bear. Come on down. He's waiting for you."

Faith practically ran for the library doors, only to find herself face-to-face with Chief Garris. "Good morning," he said.

"Afternoon, actually," Faith said. "Did you need me? I was about to run downstairs to find some lunch."

"I just wanted to let you know that Mr. Venn still hasn't regained consciousness," the chief said. "Apparently there's some swelling on his brain from being bashed in the head. It doesn't look good."

"Oh," Faith said softly. "Oh, I'm so sorry to hear that. He seemed like such a nice guy." Then she looked at the chief quizzically.

"You came all the way over here to tell me that?"

The chief shook his head. "Not that it isn't a pleasure to chat with you, but I'm here to see Wolfe Jaxon and Marlene Russell up on the third floor. I stopped here on my way up."

Faith smiled slightly. "Not stalling, are you?"

"I never put off seeing Mr. Jaxon."

But Marlene is a totally different story, Faith thought. "You have my sympathy. I do have to run though or I'm going to miss out on lunch entirely. Good luck with your meeting."

"Thanks." He stepped out of her way and she began the walk down the long gallery hall with the chief at her side. He looked sideways at her. "By the way, did you happen to get any revelations about why Venn might have been lurking outside your cottage in the dark?"

She shook her head. "No. The only conversations we'd ever had were about work, and they were always friendly. I don't know why he would have come to see me. Or why someone might have hurt him. The person couldn't have confused him with me, even in the dark."

"I agree. Though I suppose he could have come upon someone trying to break into your cottage and tried to intervene."

"I didn't see any sign of a break-in."

"I sent one of my officers over to check the doors and windows and the area around the cottage in the daylight. Maybe he'll find something. I know I'd like to get some answers. You let me know if you think of anything that might help, even if it seems inconsequential. At this point, I'm more than willing to entertain any ideas."

"If I think of something, I'll let you know right away."

"I'd appreciate anything that helps sort this mess out. Well, you have a nice lunch." He veered off toward the grand staircase, and Faith walked on to the more utilitarian stairs going down to the basement.

Brooke grabbed her the moment she came off the stairs. "It's about time you got down here. Marlene is gone, so you should be safe," she whispered, half-dragging Faith down the hall and into the baker's kitchen, where a few people looked up from their work. Brooke waved at them as she towed Faith through the room.

"She's upstairs having a meeting with Wolfe and the police chief," Faith said after they passed the bakers and were nearing the back of the room.

Brooke looked at her in approval. "Your spy skills are impressive."

"Not really. I ran into the chief. That's what held me up."

Brooke opened a door at the back of the room and cool air greeted them. They walked into the softly lit storeroom where Liam Ahlberg leaned against a pallet stacked with huge bags of flour. He sipped from a mug of coffee, then raised it in greeting toward Faith. "Hi. What's with all the cloak and dagger?"

"Sorry," Faith said. "I didn't mean to be mysterious. I only wanted to talk to you without getting you in trouble with your boss."

"No worries." He took another long sip of coffee and gave Brooke a pitiful sad-eyed look. "I am missing lunch though."

"I'll go grab you something," Brooke said. "Can't have you fainting from hunger until Faith is done pumping you for information." She turned and slipped out of the pantry.

Liam laughed. "That one is having entirely too much fun. She reminds me a bit of my wife. She's always up for an adventure too." He looked at Faith curiously. "You really didn't need to go to all this trouble. Elton isn't that bad. I would have chatted with you in the break room."

"And rob Brooke of all this entertainment? Besides, *my*

boss has made this conversation off-limits, so it's better if we chat privately." She looked at him curiously. "How is Elton to work for?"

He shrugged. "Haven't we covered this subject before?"

"Yes, but I guess I'm trying to dig a little deeper."

"Suit yourself. Well, let's see what I can say. Producers can be challenging, but Elton's not the worst of the lot. He's quick to give praise and to acknowledge he doesn't make the show single-handedly. That's unusual in this business."

"He must be upset about the show ending."

"He's not happy about it. None of us are, since it'll mean hustling for new jobs, though I don't think any of us will be out of work long. There's lots of television to be made. Of course, Elton comes out of it better than most."

"Oh?"

"He's got a residuals deal, so with the show going into syndication, especially overseas, he's going to make plenty. He can be picky about what projects he takes on with that nice nest egg to keep him comfortable."

"So he's not mad at Sugar about it?"

"Not so I can see. I don't know why he would be."

Well, there's one suspect down. Faith made one last jab at the subject. "How do Elton and Sugar get along?"

"Two high-strung divas who each think the popularity of the show is entirely due to their own brilliance? About as well as you'd imagine. They are scrupulously polite to each other, then mutter darkly afterward, but it's nothing big. Nothing I haven't seen on a dozen other projects."

Faith finally gave up on the topic while Liam took another opportunity to sip his coffee. "Do you know Cole Venn?"

A smile bloomed across the big man's face. "Sure. I know

Cole." Then his grin faded. "I felt bad about what happened. He's young and impulsive, but he's not a bad sort."

Faith assumed Liam meant the attack and wondered how Liam had learned about Cole's injury so quickly. "I'm sure he'll be okay."

"Yeah, of course, he found this sweet job," Liam said gesturing toward the ceiling. "And I think he likes it here, but it's definitely not the plan Cole had for his life."

Faith was totally confused. "What was Cole's life plan?"

"Ultimately, he wanted to be a director, and he made some cool indie stuff when Elton wasn't working him to death."

Realization dawned on Faith. "Cole worked on *Sweet & Sassy*."

Now it was Liam's turn to look confused. "Yeah, of course. That's how I knew him. He was doing a great job too, which must have made it even more painful when he got fired."

"What did he get fired for?" Faith asked.

Liam suddenly looked uncomfortable. "None of this gets back to your boss, okay? I don't want to be the cause of Cole losing this job."

"I'm not planning to tell her."

"Well, you've met Sugar. You know how she is. She flirts with every man she comes across. It's like breathing for her. She's done it to me, and I'm a married man. But Cole is younger, and he took her seriously. I tried to warn him, but he was smitten good and proper."

"What happened?"

"He got up the courage and asked Sugar out. She flatly told him that she was not going to date him, ever. She doesn't date 'the help.'"

"Ouch."

"You got that right. He was furious. Anyway, he keyed her

car." Liam held up a hand. "I know, I wouldn't support that kind of behavior either. He was way out of line. And he was also stupid. He keyed the car right in front of the parking lot security cameras. As you might imagine, that was the end of Cole's tenure with *Sweet & Sassy*."

"He must have nursed a big grudge against Sugar."

"For a while, maybe, but he had to realize he brought all that on himself. I wasn't the only one who warned him he was spinning fantasies out of a little flirting. I haven't really had a chance to talk to him this week, but he seems to be in a good place. I think he'll be okay. It might be awhile before he works in the business again, but showbiz is known for having a short memory. If he gives it some time, he could come back, especially once *Sweet & Sassy* is wrapped."

"How did you know Cole was working here?"

"I saw him one day, rushing around. We didn't have long to talk and he asked me not to mention his past to anyone. I think maybe his boss doesn't know the real reason he left his last position, so I'd appreciate it if you kept it between the two of us. Cole made a really stupid mistake, and I'm not defending him for it, but a man's got to make a living, you know?"

Faith nodded. "Did any of the other crew know Cole was here?"

"I don't know. No one mentioned it." He peered into his empty coffee cup in dismay. "You suppose Brooke got lost bringing me something to eat?"

"I'm sure she'll be here in a moment, though you can go back to the break room if you want. I don't have any other questions."

"Okay. Hey, if you see Cole, tell him I'd love to go grab a beer with him after the wrap. We could catch up."

"I'll tell him if I have a chance to talk to him." Faith didn't want to be the one to pass along the bad news about Cole's attack.

She watched Liam amble out of the pantry, and she stood for a moment mulling over the things he'd told her. Cole had a very good reason to be mad at Sugar. A lovelorn person might consider it fate that the woman he blamed for the loss of his job showed up at his new job. Plus, Cole was a redhead, which could mean he was the one she saw on the balcony on the day of the first "accident." But if Cole was the one trying to kill Sugar, who was the one who had tried to kill Cole?

19

Faith walked down the long gallery hall, her thoughts whirling. She felt as if she'd picked up a few more puzzle pieces in her chat with Liam, but she still wasn't certain where they fit. She paused under the statue of Agatha Christie and looked up at the writer's likeness, who gazed over Faith's head with a contemplative expression. "I could use a little of your talent for solving mysteries right about now," Faith said.

Agatha had nothing to say, so Faith walked on into the library. The room was nearly as empty as before, though Faith was surprised to see Watson perched on her desk, looking very smug. "How did you get in here?"

Chief Garris stepped out of the alcove near the spiral staircase, holding a small pile of papers. "I let him in. He was outside with his nose pressed against the door glass when I came in looking for you." He held up a small bundle of papers. "I needed to make a copy, and I remembered that you had a hidden copy center down here."

"It's not hidden, it's discreet," Faith said.

"You know, your boss said something almost exactly like that when she complained about the guests seeing too many police officers on the property. She suggested they change out of their uniforms before answering calls here, for the sake of discretion."

"I'm sure that suggestion was well received."

"As you'd imagine."

"Actually, I'm really glad you came back to the library before leaving. I had a meeting of my own, and I'd like to talk to you about it."

The chief raised his eyebrows. "A meeting? Are you due for a little talk about leaving the investigating to the police?"

"Do you want to hear about this?"

"Fine. Consider yourself lectured and tell me what you know."

Now that she had his attention, Faith took a moment to sort out her thoughts. She stroked Watson's warm fur to help settle her nerves. "I had a talk with Liam Ahlberg. He's on the *Sweet & Sassy* film crew. He knows Cole Venn."

Again the chief raised his eyebrows, but this time he didn't say anything.

"Apparently Cole worked on the show's crew until he lost his job after an incident related to Sugar. He may have blamed Sugar for his termination." Faith's fingers quit curling into Watson's fur long enough to make the cat grumble. She forced her hands to relax. "What if Cole is the one who tried to kill Sugar?"

"Sounds like Cole Venn deserves some scrutiny, though that was going to happen anyway because of the attack. Still, we found the poison in Andrew Ashe's room."

"Cole works here, and he's very personable. I don't think he'd have much trouble getting one of the housekeeping staff to let him into a room, no matter how much it's against the rules."

"You met him," the chief said. "What were your impressions of him?"

Faith hugged Watson to her chest. "I liked him. Which makes me worry about my character judgment if it turns out he nearly killed me twice."

"Bad guys often don't seem very bad at all," the chief said. "If Venn is the one who's trying to kill Sugar, we still need to figure out who tried to kill Venn. Which makes me wonder if Ashe knew Cole Venn used to work for *Sweet & Sassy* and now works here. If he made the same connections you have, I definitely need to have another chat with him. He may have gone after Venn, either because he hoped Venn would take the fall for the attempts on Miss Worthington or because Cole Venn actually did try to kill Sugar and frame Ashe."

"You haven't talked to Andrew Ashe yet about Cole?"

"We're having trouble finding him. But we will."

Before Faith could come up with a response, two women strode into the library, caught sight of her and hurried over. "I'll leave you to your work," the chief said, "while I go do mine."

He left as the women reached Faith. "I don't remember seeing him at the resort before," the shorter of the two guests, a silver-haired woman with glasses, whispered. "He's good-looking."

"He is," Faith agreed pleasantly. "And I'm sure his wife thinks so too."

"Married." The woman sighed. "All the good ones are."

Her friend laughed. "I personally never let reality interfere with my appreciation of a good-looking man. Though I do like a man with a bit more hair."

Faith wondered what Chief Garris would think of the discussion of his physical attributes. Though he always looked neat, she suspected the chief didn't give that much thought to how attractive he was. "Can I help you ladies with something?"

The taller of the two women sighed. "You could make the retreat last another week. I've grown very fond of all this luxury."

"That's easy to do. I'm glad you've enjoyed it."

Her friend spoke up. "We wanted to know if you have any recipes in your collection that feature quinoa. We had a wonderful quinoa salad at lunch yesterday, and I'd love to make something like that when I get home."

"I definitely have some recipe books that would feature that ingredient," Faith said. "I can also see about getting you the recipe for the Castleton Manor salad. Our chef is very generous with recipes that way."

"Thank you." The woman clapped her hands in delight, startling Watson, who squirmed in Faith's arms. She set him down gently on the desk. Faith pulled out her phone and called Brooke.

"Brooke's Clandestine Events," her friend said. "How may I help you?"

Faith laughed. "You are a fine event planner. This time I need something a little less mysterious. I have a couple of guests up here in the library, and they wonder if they could get the recipe for the quinoa salad from yesterday."

"Hey, that's one of mine," Brooke said. "I'm so glad they liked it. Sure, do you want me to recite it over the phone or should I write it down and run it up to you?"

"Whichever is easier for you."

Brooke sighed. "Since I have already been shirking a little this morning, it's probably better if I recite it. Though I would love to come up and pump you for details after your talk with Liam."

Faith leaned over her desk to grab a notepad. "I promise to catch you up later. For now, I've got a notepad, and I'm ready when you are."

With the two women reading over her shoulder and commenting on each ingredient, Faith found it challenging to transcribe the recipe as Brooke recited it. But she managed to get it all down and read it back to make sure she got it right, then promised again to update Brooke soon before ending the call.

"Do you still want to see more cookbooks?" Faith asked as the two women read through their recipes happily. They looked up and bobbed their heads in such perfect unison that it made Faith smile. She led them back to the cookbook section and began making recommendations.

Apparently the two women had primed the pump for resort guests to pop in to get a last look at the resort's cookbook collection. Faith stayed busy finding recipes and making recommendations, then watching as the guests hand-copied the recipes. Some of the books simply wouldn't stand up to the rough handling needed for scanning or photocopying. For the newer books, Faith preferred not to put the books through that when recipes were fairly easy to write down. None of the guests objected, since they were all cookbook lovers themselves.

It seemed as if the library would never clear out, but Faith didn't have the heart to rush anyone. The guests would have to leave the beautiful library and resort soon enough. She knew the end of any retreat was bittersweet. The guests were both sad to be leaving and eager to go home energized and refreshed.

Faith kept the library open a bit late to accommodate the last two guests, who were perfectly willing to don cotton gloves so they could gently look through some of the rare vintage cookbooks. Finally they both had seen all they wanted—or chose to have mercy on Faith, who must have looked as tired and hungry as she felt—and they thanked her profusely before they left.

"Watson?" Faith called. "Where are you? It's time to go home."

A black-and-white head poked out from under the love seat near the room's large fireplace. Watson looked around the room for a moment before he finally gave in to Faith's coaxing and slithered out. Faith scooped him up and chucked him under the chin. "Was all the bustle disturbing your afternoon nap schedule?"

"You're still here!"

Faith turned toward the door where Brooke stood beaming at her. "I was certain you'd be gone but I had to check. Can I talk you into giving me the details of the case?"

Faith gave her friend a look of mild disapproval. "A case is something the police have. And I would never interfere."

"Of course not." Brooke didn't sound the least bit repentant. "So, are you going to spill the details or not?"

"Let's go out to the terrace. I want to close up the library before I get any more guests looking for recipes." Brooke waited patiently while Faith finished up, then they walked out to the shadowy terrace. The air was chilly, but Faith had dressed for it. She walked over and sat on one of the benches, carefully choosing one that wasn't under the upstairs balcony. She sat stroking Watson, who seemed content to sit in her warm lap.

"Liam knows Cole, though he doesn't know about the attack." Faith paused, then amended her statement. "At least he didn't know about it this morning. I imagine the Castleton Manor gossip chain has probably reached him by now. Apparently Cole used to work for *Sweet & Sassy*."

"The plot thickens."

"It gets positively chunky," Faith said. "Cole apparently took Sugar's flirting seriously. He lost his job with the television show after Sugar rejected him. He took out his hard feelings on her car."

"So do you think he's the one who tried to hurt Sugar and you?"

"I don't know. I liked him. He seemed so sweet. But then again, I didn't see his hot-tempered side." Faith's hand stilled on the cat's fur, so Watson twisted to butt his head against her hand.

"Did you tell the chief all this?"

"Yes. He still thinks maybe Ashe attacked Cole."

"Why would he do that?"

"Revenge, maybe. If Cole was the one attacking Sugar, then he must have framed Ashe."

Brooke pulled the collar of her jacket up. "What do you think?"

"I don't know. It's a theory that makes sense of all the pieces of the puzzle, but it's almost too convenient."

"Maybe." Brooke shivered. "As much as I love all this intrigue, I'm going to go get in my car and blast the heater. It's too cold for me to deduce."

Watson must have agreed, or else he was annoyed with Faith for not petting him, because he squirmed from her lap and stalked across the terrace. "Apparently Watson is ready to head home too. I have to admit, I'm looking forward to a quiet evening in front of the fire with a book."

"Sounds good," Brooke said. "Maybe choose something besides a mystery."

The two parted and Faith followed Watson along the path to the cottage. As much as she wanted to close herself in for the night, she wondered if she should drive over to the hospital to visit Cole. Not being family, they probably wouldn't let her in to see him. And if he was still unconscious, there wouldn't be any real benefit of the drive except to make her day a little longer.

Plus, if Cole was the one who had tried to hurt her, should she even consider getting close to him, unconscious or not? Still, as much as she knew the puzzle pieces fit the new theory well, she couldn't set aside the fact that she'd liked Cole. She thought of how good he'd been with Watson and with Sugar's dogs. He seemed so kindhearted and patient. How could he have fooled her so completely?

Faith looked around the path ahead and realized she couldn't see Watson. "Rumpy?" she called out. "If you wander off, you're going to miss dinner."

The cat didn't appear, and Faith kept walking. Watson knew the way back and forth from the cottage better than she did. But she wanted him with her so she didn't feel quite so alone on the dark path. To her relief, she saw him slip out from between two potted chrysanthemums on the path ahead.

She was nearing the end of the summer gardens. The path forked in front of her, and she turned down the fork that led through the Victorian garden, the last of the formal gardens before she reached her cottage.

A dogwood tree with its gold and red leaves turned to gray by the shadowy darkness stood near the edge of the Victorian garden. A thicker shadow seemed to pull free from the tree and step into the puddle of light from one of the path lamps. Faith gasped as she recognized the man walking toward her, a furious expression on his face.

It was Andrew Ashe.

20

As the young man walked toward her, Faith yelped and backed away until she felt the soft bump of Watson against one ankle. She held up both hands.

At her obvious fear, Andrew's expression changed. He stopped and held up his own hands. "It's okay. I'm not here to hurt anyone." In the pool of light, he looked tired and ragged and a lot less ominous.

Faith took another step backward, pushing the cat a little with her foot, still wary though annoyance was starting to overtake fear. "Lurking in the dark is a terrific way to show your peaceful intent."

"I'm sorry about scaring you." He ran a hand over his cropped curls, then shoved it into the pocket of the hoodie that he wore. "I just want to clear my name."

"That would probably be easier if the police hadn't found a bottle of poison in your room."

Andrew took another step forward, nearly shouting as he pointed at her. "That wasn't mine."

Faith backed away some more. *Wrong tactic. Don't work the guy up.* She needed to keep the young man calm and hope someone stumbled upon them so she wasn't alone with someone who was possibly a felon. Not that anyone was likely to be wandering in the Victorian garden on a cold night.

"Why would someone try to frame you for the attempt on Sugar's life?" Faith asked, keeping her tone soothing, she hoped.

"Because I was easy," he grumbled, stuffing his hand back into his jacket pocket. "Everyone knew I was mad at Sugar.

And I had a right to be. She stole recipes from my collection, and now I can't use them in my own cookbook. Everybody knows I was Sugar's protégé. If I put out something with the same recipes as Sugar's new cookbook, everyone will think I'm copying her. Those are old family recipes. It's like giving up a part of my heritage."

Faith slipped both hands into her own jacket pockets and felt her phone. She wondered if she should try to call someone, though she doubted Andrew would react well if a voice came out of her coat. Plus, to be honest, she wanted to hear what Andrew had to say. "You know, stalking me in the dark doesn't help your case."

He groaned and walked over to the stone bench inside the Victorian garden and flopped down on it. "It doesn't matter. I know how guilty I look, but I didn't do anything wrong. And I definitely couldn't have gotten into Sugar's room to leave that candy. Plus, I was locked up during the attack near the stables."

"How did you know about that?"

"I was questioned about it this afternoon." He kicked absently at the mulch around the bench with the heel of his shoe. "I think the chief believes I have an accomplice. He certainly acted like it. But I don't. I'm not a killer. I'm a baker."

"I don't know that the two are mutually exclusive."

"In my case, they are."

Faith had to admit that the young man didn't look very dangerous now. He mostly looked lost and defeated. "It's the whole motive thing," she said. "There is no doubt you had plenty of motive."

"Sure, I was mad at her. But there's a big difference between being mad at someone and trying to poison that person. I don't hate Sugar. She actually helped me a lot as a chef. I looked up to her. That's why it hurt so much when she stole from me. I still feel betrayed. But I'm not the only person who is mad at Sugar Worthington."

"Like Cole Venn."

Andrew blinked at her, surprised at the name. "That's the guy from the TV crew who keyed her car, right?" He shook his head. "I remember him. He had it bad for Sugar, but I tried to tell him that she flirted with everyone." He huffed. "She flirted with *me*. I just had sense enough not to take it seriously."

"But he didn't listen to you."

"He didn't listen to anyone. Some of the other guys on the crew tried to tell him too. Cole was sure the way she talked to him was special. He believed it right up until Sugar put the smackdown on him, poor guy."

"I don't know that I feel *that* sorry for him. He did key her car."

Andrew winced. "Yeah, and it was a *nice* car. A vintage Jag and sweet. I don't know how a guy could mess up a car like that."

"A really angry guy."

He shrugged. "Sure, he was mad, but I can't see him trying to kill her over it. I mean, he had months to get over it. He probably has a job by now."

"He does. Here at Castleton Manor."

Wide-eyed, Andrew gave a low whistle. "So why is the chief still bugging me? Sounds like he ought to chat up Cole."

"He would," Faith said. "Except that Cole is in the hospital after someone bashed him in the head."

"You think I did that too? Am I going to be hounded for everything that happens at this resort? I didn't even know Cole worked here, and I've got no reason to hurt him. None."

"Unless he's the one who framed you for the attacks on Sugar."

"I didn't even know he was here," Andrew repeated. He shook

his head over and over. "Look, Cole was mad about the flirting, and probably none too happy about being fired, but if he got a job here . . ." He motioned with his hand to take in the beautiful gardens around him. "It looks like he landed on his feet. He'd have to be some kind of psycho to still carry that grudge, and Cole always seemed like a nice guy."

"I've heard people say that about serial killers." Still, Faith had more than a few of her own doubts. Sure, Cole and Andrew *looked* like good suspects. But neither one *felt* like a good suspect. As she pondered what Andrew had said, she watched Watson trot over and hop up onto the bench beside the young man. Andrew began petting him.

Well, Watson doesn't seem to think he's a killer. Not that Faith was about to trust the cat's judgment unreservedly. "If not Cole, then you're the only other person we know with motive."

"Lame motive," Andrew said as Watson stepped up into the young man's lap so Andrew could continue petting him. Stroking the cat seemed to have a calming effect on Andrew as his voice grew less strained. "Sure, I don't like what Sugar did, and I wanted to tell people about it, but that's as far as it got. I'll come up with more recipes to finish the book. Maybe I'll even do some new twist on the ones Sugar stole and include them anyway. I wouldn't be much of a chef if I couldn't overcome this. I wanted to use my grandma's recipes, but I wouldn't kill someone."

"So we have two suspects with weak motives. What we need is someone with a stronger motive. Who has an actual reason to kill Sugar? What do you know about her fans? I understand some of them have been fairly unhappy with her."

"The weight loss thing?" he asked. "I don't know about fans. They can be crazy sometimes, but you're talking about a whole series of attacks. That sounds too calculated for a loony fan."

"What do you think of the relationship between Sugar and Mitzi?" Faith asked.

He brightened visibly at that. "I don't think it's as good as Sugar thinks it is. You think Mitzi could be a killer? She is a little kooky."

"She seems devoted."

"Mitzi is complicated. I think any devotion she might have felt was seriously diluted when Mitzi broke up with her fiancé over Sugar."

"Her fiancé? How did Sugar figure into that?"

Andrew snorted. "How does Sugar figure into anything? She flirted with him every time he showed up. At first, Mitzi laughed it off, but over time, the guy was starting to make calf eyes over Sugar. I don't think anything actually happened. Sugar never follows through on the flirting, but Mitzi and the guy fought about it . . . a lot."

"Did Sugar back off when she saw the flirting was causing trouble?"

"Sugar can't see anything that doesn't benefit Sugar," Andrew said as he continued to pet the cat. "Plus, I don't think she knows any other way to relate to men. I think flirting is like a default setting for her. She can't help herself. But apparently Mitzi thought Sugar kept it up on purpose."

That certainly made Mitzi's warnings about Wolfe make sense. Of course, Faith had no particular claim on Wolfe Jaxon. But if Mitzi was sensitive to Sugar's flirting, she might have read her own past into Faith's simple friendship with Wolfe.

"I can see how that would sour their relationship, but murder seems a little extreme," Faith said.

"I don't begin to understand women, so I can't help you with that. I've seen some pretty hot fights in my life when two women are after the same man."

"But Sugar and Mitzi aren't after the same man," Faith said. "You told me Mitzi and her fiancé broke up. If she was going to go after Sugar, it seems like she would have done it while Sugar was flirting with the guy."

"I don't know. Mitzi lets things stew. But it makes as much sense as me killing someone over a bunch of recipes, or Cole doing it because he had to change jobs. We were all pretty miffed, but no one is exactly suffering."

"Anyone else you can think of with a better motive?"

He shook his head. "I figure the network can't be happy with Sugar's decision to quit the show, but that all came after I left, so I don't know. And besides, a hitman on the film crew is more far-fetched than any of the other theories."

Faith shook her head. "I talked to one of the other crewmen and he didn't think any of the crew were really upset about the end of the series. And Fritsch is coming out on top because of residuals from syndication. As far as I can tell, he has less motive than anyone."

"Residuals aren't the same as steady work." He sighed and rubbed his hands on his legs. "So we're back to the network putting a hit out on her."

"Why would putting a hit out on her help anything? She obviously couldn't make any more shows if she was dead, so they wouldn't be any better off. At least if she was still alive she might change her mind."

"Look, I don't know. I only know I didn't try to kill Sugar. I didn't drop any flowerpots or send poisoned candy to anyone, and I sure don't have any accomplices. I'm just a baker." Since he had stopped petting Watson, the cat had hopped down from the bench and was sniffing around the plants. "Will you mention Mitzi to the police chief? Give him someone other than me to focus on? That's all I ask."

"I think the chief is focused on Cole at the moment," Faith said. "Though he has some interest in how you might be connected to Cole. I don't suppose anyone saw you right after you left the police station. The chief said you were hard to track down."

"Well, I wasn't about to come back here. I was given every reason to believe that doing so would be a huge mistake," Andrew said. "Though I should at least pick up my stuff. I booked a room in town at the little bed-and-breakfast near the water. There's no way I could just turn up here and expect a warm welcome."

"Booking a room is something at least. It shows you weren't on the grounds at that time, anyway. You said you were questioned. I take it you got the impression you're still a suspect."

Andrew groaned. "That chief is sizing me up for a prison uniform. I could tell. Right now, I just want to go home and forget everything about this week." He stood and Faith tensed slightly as he brushed absently at the seat of his blue jeans before looking at her. "I'm sorry I scared you."

"It's been a jumpy week for me," Faith said. "Whatever happens, I think the chief isn't interested in arresting an innocent man. Try not to worry too much."

He nodded wearily. "I will. Thanks for listening to me and thanks for the pep talk."

"You have to believe the chief doesn't want to lock up just anyone. He wants to find the real culprit."

"I hope you're right." He bobbed his head at her one more time before heading off into the darkness. As soon as Andrew was out of sight, Watson popped out of the brush and began weaving between Faith's ankles. She leaned over and scooped him up. "Thanks for being my hero," she said as she rubbed his head. "You know, a dog would have stayed by my side and growled at Andrew, not sat in his lap." Watson just purred in response, clearly not the least bit guilty.

She carried the cat through the Victorian garden and up the path to the cottage. To her relief, nothing else jumped out at her and no one lay sprawled near the cottage. Still, she kept a good grip on Watson as she unlocked the cottage door and slipped in. She had no interest in chasing the cat around in the darkness.

Once inside, she built a quick fire and pulled a small casserole out of the freezer to pop into the oven. It was one Brooke had taught her to make, and now Faith had added it to her mass cooking days when she would whip up pots of soup and casseroles, then divide them into individual portions and freeze them. It helped her avoid the temptation to lean on packaged food on nights when work had worn her out.

Watson wolfed down his own dinner and was asleep in Faith's chair by the fire by the time she walked over to sit with her dinner. She didn't bother to push the cat to one side, as that would have resulted in a battle for chair space and Faith was too tired for that. She carried her dish to the table instead, pulled her laptop toward her, and turned it on.

While watching the computer start up, she took several bites of the luscious creamy casserole, enjoying the mildly spiced rotisserie chicken, sautéed vegetables, and cheese sauce, then she clicked on her search engine. She had already checked out Sugar's fans on the discussion boards, but she wondered if the Internet could offer her information on any of the other people involved.

She typed in *Mitzi Hubert* and found references to her in connection with Sugar. She was mostly an inside source when reporters wanted to write about the pastry chef, but nothing was focused on Mitzi herself. The quotes from the personal assistant were all the sort of fluff you might expect. Sugar cared deeply about her fans. Sugar believed in balance in everything. Sugar was looking forward to this event or that. But there was frustratingly little to give real insight into either woman or their relationship.

On a whim, she decided to do a search on Elton Fritsch and looked through his list of accomplishments. Because Faith didn't watch a lot of TV, the list wasn't very meaningful, but she could tell that *Sweet & Sassy* was the show for which he was best known. The next-biggest credit seemed to be a reality TV show about movie stuntmen, but that series hadn't lasted long. Faith wished she'd known about that one. It might have been interesting to watch.

Faith shoved another bite of casserole into her mouth and began looking for more personal information on Fritsch. He seemed to live a work-focused life, and she found no sign of anything scandalous. He had responded to one interview about *Sweet & Sassy* where he said Sugar was as delightful to work with as she was to watch. "Which suggests he's comfortable with lying to the public," she said to Watson. Not that Sugar had seemed *hard* to work with, but clearly her flirting was an issue behind the scenes.

Faith paused in raising another bite to her mouth. She'd heard about Sugar flirting with the crew and with Mitzi's fiancé and she'd seen the woman flirt with Wolfe, but how about Fritsch? Had he ever been the target of a full-on Sugar Worthington flirt fest? And if so, how had he reacted to that? Could he be carrying some kind of torch for Sugar? That might have made him particularly upset when she decided to leave him by leaving the show. Of course, that would also make him certifiably unhinged. Pretty much all of the motives she'd found for anyone required the person to respond to minor issues with over-the-top violence. Even if Fritsch was smitten with Sugar, that hardly seemed a motive for murder, or at least not a more impressive motive than losing a job or having recipes stolen.

She flatly couldn't find anyone who would actually benefit from Sugar's death. And wasn't that really the key? Who would feel their life was better if Sugar lost hers? Faith let out a long theatrical sigh that made her chuckle at herself afterward. She poked at her empty dish and decided to have a bowl of ice cream for dessert. She might not have any answers, but at least she could drown her feelings of defeat in comfort food.

21

Shortly before dawn, Faith sat bolt upright as she woke from a horrific dream about a faceless attacker trying to suffocate her. Watson tumbled into her lap from where he'd been sprawled across her chest. Through the bedclothes, he sunk his claws into her thigh as he squirmed to his feet.

"Ouch," Faith said. She lifted the cat from her lap and set him onto the bed beside her. "No wonder I was having nightmares. My cat was trying to suffocate me. You know, that's why no one calls you man's best friend."

Watson gave her an annoyed look, then turned his back on her and began his morning grooming.

Though it was technically her day off, Faith knew there was no point trying to go back to sleep. She definitely didn't want to revisit her dream, and she was wide awake. She slipped out of bed and headed for the shower, hoping to drive the last remnants of the disturbing dream away with hot water.

After the shower and a leisurely breakfast, Faith set about cleaning the cottage, doing all the vacuuming and dusting that she usually scheduled for her days off. She found her thoughts turning again and again toward Sugar and Cole and Andrew. Though the cookbook retreat was over as far as the guests were concerned, Faith wasn't sure the danger that had arrived with them was gone. Someone had tried to kill Sugar three times and had sent Cole to the hospital. Faith could see no reason why the person would quit trying. As the swirl of possible suspects raced through her head, she turned again and again to Mitzi and her clear bitterness toward Sugar about her fiancé. Though Faith had questioned Andrew's theories about Mitzi, she had to admit that Sugar's assistant wasn't the person she wanted people to believe she was. Mitzi tried hard to sound like she loved her boss, but Faith had seen more than enough evidence to suggest that she felt just the opposite.

She managed to stay on task through the vacuuming, but her worry simply wouldn't let her focus. *I'll walk over to the manor and make sure Sugar is okay*, she told herself. *And maybe find out if Marlene has any news on Cole.* She cringed inwardly at the thought of another talk with Marlene. She wondered if she could try calling the chief. She could tell him about her chat with Andrew and get an update on the case. She wasn't sure he'd be any more thrilled to talk to her than would Marlene, but he'd probably be less unpleasant.

As soon as she opened her door, Watson dashed outside, nearly tripping her along the way. He raced ahead of her down the path, then stopped and looked back at her, as if taunting her lack of speed. "You know, one of these days I'm going to look up the statistics on how many people are killed by their cats," she said, wagging a finger at him. "After last night, I'm beginning to get distinctly suspicious."

Watson merely turned and continued up the path. The night's chill was beginning to dissipate in the warm sunshine, and it looked like it was going to be a beautiful day. Faith wondered if she should drive into town later and do some shopping while the weather was so lovely. Maybe it would stop the swirl of worry in her mind.

As she walked up the steps to the front doors, she saw guests coming out, wheeling luggage across the tiled terraces and looking refreshed. The sight of the smiling faces and the sound of the warm greetings Faith received as each person passed reminded her that Castleton Manor truly was a wonderful place. They'd had some trouble during the week, but that had been only a small portion of an otherwise enjoyable stay. That sense of perspective finally began to lessen the grip of Faith's frayed nerves.

"Excuse me?"

Faith turned to look into a smiling, round face that she recognized. She'd seen the guest several times in the library. "Yes?"

The woman smiled a bit shyly. "I wanted to thank you for your talk on antique cookbooks. And the way you shared recipes with us. I really feel so charged up and ready to work on my own cookbook."

"I'm so glad. Thank you for sharing that with me."

Buoyed with good feelings, Faith headed through the doors and immediately spotted another familiar face, actually two of them. She hurried across the entry toward her friend Midge, who stood cuddling her tiny Chihuahua. Atticus wore his Doggles, as usual, and this time they were matched with a faux-leather jacket and tiny scarf.

"Atticus is looking adventurous today," Faith said.

"This is last year's Halloween outfit," Midge said. "He was Snoopy as a flying ace. This week he is wearing all his past costumes in preparation for Halloween."

Faith looked at her friend in surprise. She'd totally forgotten it was almost Halloween. "I don't suppose I'll be getting many trick-or-treaters at the cottage. I loved giving out treats when I lived in Boston. I miss that."

"Do you miss Boston a lot?" Midge asked.

"Not most of the time." Faith sighed. "I do miss having lunch at Faneuil Hall Marketplace sometimes. You could find anything there."

"Well, you don't have to miss trick-or-treating," Midge said. "I'm having Yip-or-Treat at Happy Tails on Halloween night. You and Watson should come over and help me pass out goodies. Some of the costumes are adorable."

"That sounds like fun, though I seriously doubt I could get Watson into a costume," Faith said.

Midge seemed to think about that for a moment. "You could put a bow tie on him. With his tuxedo markings, he'd look very debonair."

"I might be able to manage that," Faith said. "Do I have to dress up too?"

"You don't *have* to," Midge said. "You *get* to. How many other chances do we get to play dress-up? You'd have to think of some costume that works with a tuxedo." She tapped a finger on her cheek. "I'm sure we could come up with something. We should ask Brooke. She has a great imagination for that sort of thing. She's the one who came up with the idea for Atticus's costume this year."

"Oh? What's his costume?"

"It's a surprise, but I can tell you since you inspired it."

"I did?"

"Indirectly, Watson actually did." Midge gave her a mischievous smile. "Atticus is going to be Sherlock Holmes. See? That's why you have to bring Watson."

Faith looked at the friendly little dog, picturing him in a deerstalker hat and his little glasses and giggled. "That will be a surprising combination."

Midge joined in the laughter, then she looked over Faith's shoulder and her eyes grew wide. "Speaking of surprises, look who's coming over to chat with us."

Faith turned to look and felt a wash of warmth in her face

as Wolfe Jaxon strode across the foyer toward them, looking very much like a man on a mission. Faith felt a stab of worry. *Has something else dreadful happened?*

"What a nice start to my morning," Wolfe said as he reached them. "A chance to speak with two lovely ladies." He turned his attention to Midge. "I hope you're not here for any sick guests."

As the concierge vet, Midge was on-call to tend to the pets of the resort's guests, but she shook her head at Wolfe. "Not today. I came to drop off treats at the pet spa. Apparently the guests this week loved them, and I needed to restock." She dropped her voice to a conspiratorial whisper. "Though I admit, I was lingering a little. I'd hoped to catch sight of Sugar Worthington."

"She and her assistant joined me this morning for breakfast," Wolfe said, and Faith was surprised at the instant pang of jealousy she felt. "But I'm not certain where she is now."

"That's all right," Midge said. "I'm going to try to catch Brooke for a chat about Halloween costumes. It was nice to see you both." She tipped a wink at Faith, the message clear. She was leaving Faith alone with Wolfe on purpose. Midge was an incurable matchmaker, probably because she was so happily married. She wanted the same for all her friends.

Wolfe bid Midge a good day, then turned his full attention on Faith. "I'm surprised to see you here on your day off. Although I do admire your work ethic."

"I'm afraid it's less work ethic and more fretting," Faith said. "I was a little worried about Sugar, after the attack on Cole Venn and then talking to Andrew Ashe last night."

Wolfe's expression turned alarmed. "Was this conversation on the resort grounds?"

Faith nodded. "He was lurking in the Victorian garden."

"I don't like the sound of that. Are you all right?"

"I'm fine. He only wanted to talk, mostly to declare his innocence. I have to admit, he seemed sincere. He did know Cole, but he didn't seem to be aware of the attack." She related the conversation she'd had with Andrew.

"He may simply be a skilled actor," Wolfe said. "Have you spoken with Chief Garris about this meeting? Certainly he'll want to know."

"Not yet, though I intend to. Honestly, Andrew did nothing threatening, and since he left immediately I didn't think calling the chief was pressing. I was too exhausted to think straight about it."

"I'm expecting the chief this morning," Wolfe said. "I'll be sure to tell him what you've told me, and I know he'll want to speak with you about it."

"Of course. Do you happen to have any updates on Cole?"

Wolfe nodded. "There's been no change in his condition. Apparently this is a case where no news is not good news. He should have regained consciousness by now."

Faith sighed. She knew the chief suspected Cole in the attacks on Sugar, attacks that could easily have killed Faith as well, but she simply couldn't reconcile the pleasant man with that kind of violence. "You said you spoke with Sugar this morning. Does she know about Cole?"

"I told her, but I'm still not sure what she thought about it. She is a difficult person to have a serious conversation with. And to be honest, her . . . enthusiastic friendliness is rather overwhelming."

Faith was embarrassed at how glad she was to hear him say that. "I can imagine," she said. "Still, with the guests leaving, I'm wondering if whoever wants to hurt Sugar might take another shot at her."

"If what Chief Garris believes is correct, the person who wanted Sugar hurt is in the hospital himself."

"But what if the chief isn't correct?" Faith asked.

"Perhaps we should see what Miss Worthington's schedule is for these last two days of filming. Why don't you come with me to talk to her?"

Faith wondered if Wolfe's invitation was because he wanted to spend time with her or because he didn't want to be alone with Sugar. Then she decided it didn't matter. She liked both reasons. Plus, she thought, giving herself a little mental shake, she really should be focusing on their guest's safety.

They were crossing the Main Hall and heading for the stairs near the gallery when Wolfe spotted Marlene. He called out to her, and she headed for them. "We're looking for Miss Worthington," he said as soon as Marlene was in conversation range.

"As am I," Marlene said, directing the comment toward Faith so she could give her a hostile glare. "The woman is supposed to be in the salon filming her last confessionals for the show but apparently hasn't shown up."

"Confessionals?" Wolfe echoed. "Is she planning to confess to something on the air?"

Marlene waved her hands dramatically. "I have no idea, but likely not. The term *confessional* on reality television apparently means little clips of the star talking to the camera."

Wolfe continued to look confused for a moment, then simply shook his head. "I probably should have watched some of the shows in preparation for this retreat."

"I don't see why," Marlene said. "The show is ridiculous, as reality television tends to be."

"Are you looking for Sugar now?" Faith asked.

Marlene gave her a withering look. "Of course. The sooner

she finishes this filming, the sooner Castleton Manor can return to the sort of experience we're known for."

"Have you checked Miss Worthington's suite?" Wolfe asked.

"It was the first place we checked." Marlene wrinkled her nose, her expression disgusted. "All I found were those dogs of hers. Apparently Miss Worthington put several of the decorative cushions on the floor as dog beds, and the creatures have torn them up. I made a note to deduct the damage from her appearance fee."

"I'm sure you have," Wolfe said, interrupting her complaints. "Where else have you looked?"

"I've checked most of the obvious places inside the main house."

"How about downstairs?" he asked.

Marlene looked at him in shock. "Why would a guest go downstairs?"

"Our kitchens are downstairs and Miss Worthington is a chef. I imagine she might be interested in them. I recommend you check downstairs. In fact, I believe we should split up and look for Miss Worthington. Whoever finds her can alert the other two."

Marlene looked pained at the idea. "That sounds like a great deal of fuss over someone who is probably off flirting with the gardeners or some such."

"It is a great deal of *fuss* over a missing guest at Castleton Manor," Wolfe said, his tone finally turning sharp. "A guest whose well-being is very much our concern. I hope you'll keep that in mind."

Marlene's expression turned instantly apologetic. "Of course. I'll go look for her downstairs."

"I'll check outside," Faith offered.

"Good plan," Wolfe said. "I will call the stables and ask if anyone has seen Miss Worthington up there, then I'll see if she might have returned to the third floor." He shifted uncomfortably. "She seemed somewhat reluctant to leave my quarters this morning, so she may have returned to them, not knowing I wouldn't be there. We'll meet back here in fifteen minutes." He turned his direct attention on Marlene. "If no one has discovered anything, I'd like you to call a full staff meeting so we can get more people involved in the search."

Marlene nodded and turned to head for the stairs.

Faith hurried down the gallery hall, which was unusually empty following the retreat guests' departure. Faith knew the huge room would be a hive of activity in the afternoon when the staff took advantage of the chance to give the room a thorough cleaning before the next event. For now, though, it echoed with the sound of Faith's boot heels on the floor.

The library was also empty and she gave it barely a glance before walking out onto the tiled terrace outside. Sugar had shown a particular liking for the spot, and Faith looked around, hoping to see the pastry chef enjoying the morning sun on one of the benches. Instead, she saw Watson, sitting on the stone railing.

"I wondered where you'd wandered off to," Faith said. "I don't suppose you've seen Sugar."

Hopping from the railing and circling Faith's legs, Watson meowed, giving the sound the kind of urgency he usually reserved for food demands. "What's wrong? You can't be hungry already."

She bent to pick him up, but the cat wriggled through her hands and raced across the terrace. He stopped before he reached the steps and looked back at her, meowing plaintively. Feeling a little silly, Faith followed him. Following Watson had been beneficial in the past, and she really didn't have any better ideas. "You better not be leading me home for a second breakfast."

The cat trotted down the garden path, being careful to stay ahead of her. Once or twice, Faith tried to pick him up, but he darted away each time, meowing. His behavior was so odd that Faith felt increasingly concerned as they passed through the rows of potted chrysanthemums and headed for the two greenhouses that grew many of the flowers used in the beautiful arrangements throughout Castleton Manor.

The greenhouses were built from pale stone and rich red brick, with tall arched windows and towering roofs of metal and glass to let in the sunlight the plants would need. The big greenhouses were open to manor guests during the day, and Faith wondered if Sugar might have come out to check out the flowers. With most of the guests leaving, this would be a great morning for a private walk among the plants. The orchid collection was particularly lovely, and Castleton Manor was known for having developed unique strains of orchids that could be found nowhere else.

To Faith's surprise, Watson didn't slip inside the open doors of either greenhouse. Instead he passed down the narrow alley that ran between them. Faith had never even walked behind the greenhouses, so she was surprised to find a large gardener's shed, a miniature version of her own cottage, not far from where the alley opened out. Watson picked up his pace until he was running toward the shed.

"I'm not sure we're supposed to be back here," Faith said as she hurried to catch up to the cat. Then she froze. She recognized the voice coming from inside the shed. Sugar Worthington was inside, and she didn't sound happy.

22

As Faith walked closer to the shed, Sugar's voice fell silent. Faith hesitated, hoping to hear another voice, perhaps one she would recognize. Someone in the shed had clearly upset Sugar, and considering all the things that had happened in the last few days, that person's identity could be important. No one spoke, and the only sound was the dry rustle of leaves as the breeze blew a trail of them across Faith's path.

Faith took a step away from the shed. Should she call someone? She pulled her phone out of her pocket and almost groaned aloud. No signal. She wondered if something about the huge buildings right next to her could be affecting her phone.

She could turn around and go find Wolfe, but she'd feel awfully silly if it turned out Sugar was just complaining about the flowers in her room or some other innocuous thing. The more she thought about it, the more she was sure there was something about flowers in the demands Mitzi had made before Sugar's arrival. Of course, there had been so many demands.

While Faith stood debating with herself, Watson had been sniffing around the doorway to the shed. "Watson," Faith whispered when she saw the cat stretch out his neck to poke his nose into the shed. "Watson, come here."

Watson didn't even give her a glance. Instead, he padded silently into the shed. Faith waited for Sugar to exclaim over the cat, but still no sound came from inside. That silence scared Faith more than anything else. When had Sugar Worthington ever been so quiet?

Faith walked closer, making as little noise as possible on the loose gravel. The building was small compared with the towering greenhouses, but it was still nearly half the size of Faith's cottage, with the same stone walls and narrow windows.

Reaching the open door, Faith peeked in. Sugar stood in the center of the stone floor, wringing her hands. She looked up at Faith, who quickly stepped into the shed. "Are you all right?" Faith said.

Sugar's eyes were filled with tears. "I'm sorry," she whispered. "Don't move."

Before the man's words sank in, Faith had already moved, spinning around to face Elton Fritsch as he stepped out from behind the shed door and swung it shut, all the while holding a gun trained on Sugar and Faith. For a moment, all Faith could see was the gun. Despite its small size, Elton could easily kill them both.

"I'm so glad you joined us," the producer said. "I had no idea that I was going to be able to put a stop to your nosiness so easily."

His voice had finally drawn Faith's eyes upward away from the gun. The producer smirked at her, and Faith noticed that his signature scarf and knit hat were rusty red. She stared at the hat as realization swept over her. "You were wearing that hat when you tried to kill Sugar with the flowerpot. That's why I thought the person on the balcony had red hair."

His tight-lipped smile looked somehow reptilian with the cold blue eyes above it. "You're entirely too clever for your own good, Miss Newberry. I heard about your description and had to wear a different hat for most of the week. But it simply seemed appropriate to wear this again today, considering we've come full circle." He swept the hat from his head. "You don't know how disappointed I am that I'll have to get rid of this hat. It was my favorite."

"You can't imagine how sorry I am about that," Faith said drily, relieved that her voice carried no sign of trembling.

"You will be. I've made a few mistakes, but this time, I'm going with a sure thing." He waved the gun slightly for emphasis, which drew Faith's attention back to the barrel. Her stomach clenched and she wondered if this was how a bird felt when it looked into the face of the snake that would eat it.

Realizing that she was quickly spiraling into panic, Faith forced her eyes back to the producer's face. "This doesn't make any sense," she said. "Why would you kill Sugar?"

"I never did anything to him," Sugar said defensively.

The producer snorted. "She really never did. She was demanding and tiresome and always late, but I don't hold that against her. When you have a goose that lays golden eggs, you don't blame it for honking now and then."

"Then why?" Sugar wailed. "I thought we were friends."

He rolled his eyes. "Hardly. You thought I was the hired help. But this isn't about bad feelings. I don't harbor any bad feelings about you at all." He waved the gun. "Well, maybe a little annoyance at how hard you've been to kill, but that doesn't really count."

"Then why?" Faith asked, struggling to keep her voice even and calm. "If it's not personal, why go after Sugar at all?"

"Money, of course, Miss Newberry." The producer laughed. "It's always about money in the end, isn't it? And this is about lots and lots of money."

"I don't understand," Faith said. Her eyes darted to the windows and she tried to will a nice inquisitive gardener to look inside. "Is it about the syndication money?"

"You know about the syndication money? You *have* been busy. I do, in fact, receive a sizable cut of the syndication rights and Sugar has proven to be very, very popular overseas. Who would have thought?"

"So that should make up for the series ending."

He seesawed his gun back and forth. "It does and it doesn't. But you see, the syndication money came pouring in with the mystery surrounding Sugar's weight loss. Mystery and mayhem sell."

Finally Faith understood. "You figure the mysterious death of your star would skyrocket the popularity of the show."

He tapped his nose. "Bingo. You are such a smart woman. I'm almost sorry to have to kill you, but you have been a nuisance. I wonder if your death will be ignored, since you're a nobody, or if it will drive up the viewership even more. You'll be one more mystery. Too bad you'll never know one way or the other."

"Chief Garris will figure this out," Faith said.

"Oh no. Don't resort to the old clichés," he said, giving her a disappointed look, then raising his voice to a singsong falsetto. "'You'll never get away with this.'"

"Except that you won't."

"Of course I will. Your precious chief already believes he knows what happened. Cole Venn was so very hurt by Sugar's rejection that he plotted to kill her and framed poor Andrew in the process. For which Andrew attacked him." Fritsch shook his head in mock sadness. "Of course, Andrew realized it really was all Sugar's fault, so he shot her and her tiresome new friend and then fled to a nice private spot where he killed himself."

"You're planning to kill Andrew too," Faith said.

"It will make the story tidier," the producer said. "And everyone prefers a nice tidy script. Can you imagine the headlines? Betrayal, rejected lovers, and suicide. It's Hollywood gold. Maybe someone will make a movie and ask me to direct."

Sugar folded her arms over her chest. "Cole Venn was not

my lover." Her voice didn't sound scared anymore, just annoyed.

Fritsch shrugged. "It doesn't matter. The story works either way. The hotheaded young man keyed your car on video. And, of course, Miss Newberry kindly told the police that a redhead dropped a flowerpot on you both. This was a story that wrote itself. And Cole is perfect for the role of murderer."

"How many people are you going to kill for this story of yours?" Faith asked. "You're a monster."

"No, I'm a storyteller. Though you have a point. I do have a lot on my to-do list for today. Kill both of you. Kill Andrew. Make sure Cole never comes out of his coma. And be ready for my close-up as I tell everyone how very sorry I am for losing such a bright star as Sugar Worthington." He smiled at each of them. "And considering how much I have to do, I'm afraid it's time for you both to die."

The cat was bored with the gardener's shed. At first, it had been full of interesting smells, including the sharp smell of dog coming from the woman with the wild hair.

The cat had forgiven the woman for her fixation on her dogs. After all, she had always shown him the admiration he was due. Always . . . until now. He had walked right up to her and she never spoke to him at all. That's what happened to people who spent too much time with dogs. It affected their brains.

The cat didn't like the strange man. He smelled wrong. The cat had smelled that scent near his human's house, and he didn't like it then either. Plus, his human and the other nice woman smelled of fear now and he blamed the man. The cat thought the man should leave the shed. The only problem was how to get rid of him. He was so tall.

The shed did offer a nice ladder of shelves reaching nearly to the ceiling, and it didn't take the cat long to hop up to the top. He half-expected his human to object. She never liked it when he climbed on other people's things, but she didn't even look at him. Her eyes stayed on the smelly man. Another reason the man should leave.

The cat leaned far out, looking down on the man. The copper-colored circle of his knit cap was illuminated by the sunlight streaming through a nearby window. The sharp smell of fear was strong all around him. It was time to make it stop.

Elton Fritsch lifted the gun higher, pointing it first at Faith, then at Sugar, as if unsure of whom to shoot first. Faith looked around the shed, desperate for something to do, something to try, before it was too late. She didn't see anything, so she began praying silently.

Suddenly, a yowling ball of black-and-white fur launched from the top of the potting tools rack and landed right on Elton's head. The man shrieked and swatted at the clawing cat. The gun went off close to the producer's ear, making him scream again. Watson jumped lightly to the floor and sank his teeth into the man's bare ankle.

Blood ran down the producer's face and he swiped at it with one hand while hopping and trying to kick the cat. The man brought the gun back down toward the women, but before he could choose a target, Faith swung a short garden spade, slamming it into the producer's arm. He yelled and dropped the gun.

Sugar dove for the gun and quickly stood, pointing it at Elton Fritsch. "You hold it right there or I'll give you a lot more to worry about than a few scratches."

Fritsch held his arm with his free hand. "You won't shoot me."

Sugar laughed. "You forget. I'm Southern. We'll shoot anything. Deep down I never liked you, so I kinda wish you'd test me on it. As I remember, your horse trick managed to ruin my favorite pair of boots. And yes, I do hold a grudge."

"My phone won't work back here," Faith said. "I'll have to run back to the house for help. Will you be all right out here with him?"

"I'll be fine," Sugar said, her voice almost a purr. "But I can't promise my producer won't end up with a few holes if he acts up while you're gone."

Faith scooped up Watson, not wanting to leave him in case Sugar did decide to start shooting. She headed for the shed door and opened it to find Wolfe Jaxon and Chief Garris rushing in. The chief had his gun drawn, but as he looked between Sugar and the producer, he relaxed slightly. "Looks like you ladies hardly needed me at all."

"I'm the one who needs your help," Fritsch wailed. "She's trying to kill me."

"Nice try." The chief gently relieved Sugar of the gun. "We already know you're the one who tried to kill Cole Venn. You didn't hit him quite hard enough. He woke up this morning. We had a long, informative chat."

The producer swore under his breath as the chief cuffed him. Wolfe put his hand gently on Faith's arm. "Are you all right? We heard a gunshot and I nearly panicked, knowing you were outside."

She looked at him in surprise, unsure how to react to his personal concern. "I'm fine." She smiled, though it felt a little shaky. "We all are. It was a wild shot. Watson jumped on Fritsch's head and the gun went off." She pointed toward the producer. "He was going to kill us, then kill Andrew and Cole."

"But my itty-bitty hero saved us again," Sugar said as she chucked Watson under the chin. "I think this one deserves a treat."

Watson purred loudly as if he agreed with her.

"I'll take Fritsch with me," the chief said. "But I'll need a statement from you two ladies as well."

"Of course," Faith said.

"Maybe that could wait a little while," Wolfe suggested. "The ladies have been through a lot. Perhaps we could give them time to recover. I can drive them down to the station in an hour or so."

The chief agreed and while he bustled Fritsch out of the shed and across the grounds, Wolfe led Faith and Sugar back to the manor for a cup of coffee and a chance to sit down. In the quiet of one of the downstairs staff break rooms, they shared the last bits of the story. "What were you doing out at the gardener's shed?" Faith asked Sugar.

"I got a note in my room," Sugar said. "It was from Elton, saying the confessionals were going to be shot out in the gardener's shed. It seemed like a weird place, but it's not the strangest thing I've been asked to do for the show." She picked at a bit of streusel from the top of a muffin Brooke had brought to the break room for them.

"How did *you* find Sugar so fast?" Wolfe asked Faith. "You couldn't have known to check the gardener's shed."

"I didn't even know there was a shed back there. I followed Watson."

Sugar reached over to stroke Watson as he lapped up a small dollop of heavy cream, then took a delicate bite of smoked salmon in a saucer, the closest thing to a hero's reward that Brooke could come up with in the kitchen. "I certainly owe a lot to this little guy."

"And to Cole," Wolfe said. "He's the one who told the chief that Elton had attacked him."

"I'm surprised the producer let him live through the attack," Faith said. "What on earth was Cole doing at my cottage after dark?"

"He told the chief that he'd come to apologize to you and to come clean," Wolfe said. "Fritsch recognized him at the house and confronted him. Apparently Cole hadn't exactly told the truth about why he left his last job. Fritsch used that to blackmail Cole into setting the horses loose. Cole had some experience with horses in the past and Fritsch didn't. Cole said he was pretty sure the horses wouldn't actually hurt either of you, but he knew he'd put you in danger. There really is no telling what panicked horses might do."

"So Elton attacked him to keep him quiet," Faith said. "I'm surprised he didn't finish the job right then."

"I suspect you and Watson must have come along right as the attack happened," Wolfe said. "And Cole didn't see Fritsch directly at the time. He was attacked from behind. But as he fell, he recognized Fritsch's shoes. There aren't a lot of people wandering around on a cold night in Lighthouse Bay with no socks on. Plus, apparently Fritsch's shoes are distinctive."

"Fritsch's clothing choices have caused all kinds of trouble for him," Faith said.

Sugar grinned. "That's all right. Where Elton's heading, everyone wears the same thing. Prison orange!"

Learn more about Annie's fiction books at

AnniesFiction.com

- Access your e-books
- Discover exciting new series
- Read sample chapters
- Watch video book trailers
- Share your feedback

We've designed the Annie's Fiction website especially for you!

Plus, manage your account online!

- Check your account status
- Make payments online
- Update your address

Visit us at AnniesFiction.com